G. E Wyatt

Follow the right : a tale for Boys

G. E Wyatt

Follow the right : a tale for Boys

ISBN/EAN: 9783337024802

Printed in Europe, USA, Canada, Australia, Japan

Cover: Foto ©Andreas Hilbeck / pixelio.de

More available books at **www.hansebooks.com**

FOLLOW THE RIGHT

A Tale for Boys

BY

G. E. WYATT

Author of "Archie Digby," "Lionel Harcourt,"
"Harry Bertram,"
&c.

" He'd seen his duty a dead·sure thing,
And he went for it thar and then."
JOHN HAY.

London
THOMAS NELSON AND SONS
35 Paternoster Row

EDINBURGH, AND NEW YORK
1893

Contents.

FOLLOW THE RIGHT.

I.

SAVED BY THE SKIN OF HIS TEETH.

IT is the Friday before Christmas-day·in the year
188–. Windsor Station is a scene of wild confusion, and seems like a surging sea of high hats.
Look where you will, you can see nothing but boys,
boys, boys! Eton breaks up to-day, and "The holidays
have begun" is written on every face. Shouts of
laughter, very indifferent jokes, extremely familiar and
not always complimentary remarks to the porters, and
about the few passengers who have not the privilege
of being Etonians, are to be heard on all sides.

About three minutes before the train is to start, a
tall footman appears on the platform. He is followed
by an elderly lady's-maid, who holds in her arms an
enormously fat black-and-tan terrier, which, being
madly frightened, is struggling wildly for freedom.

The Eton boys instantly mark the dog and the

maid as their natural prey, and all eyes are turned upon the opening through which they have just come, to discover whose they are.   An old lady emerges hastily.   She is no thinner in proportion to her height than the animal she is following.   But if gnawing anxiety could reduce one's dimensions, she would certainly speedily become a mere shadow.   Her eyes are round with apprehension, and her face flushed with excitement.   To the infinite delight of the spectators, she comes running—positively running—after the servant, crying out as she advances,—

"Never mind, darling; was he frightened then? Ze poor 'ittle sing!—Give him to me, Watkins; do give him to me.   He isn't used to such a crush, and all these dreadful boys."

As she utters the last words the maid turns round, and in obedience to her mistress's commands delivers up the gigantic dog with an unmistakable sigh of relief.

"You must hold him tight, my lady," she says; "he's almost off his head with fright."   But her warning comes too late.   Just as the old lady takes the precious burden into her arms—I grieve to have to relate it, but pity 'tis, 'tis true—one of the Etonian spectators comes stealthily up and gives a sudden tweak to the stump of a tail which is hanging out behind.   This outrage is a last straw to the canine traveller's already overstrained powers of endurance. With a yell of mingled pain and terror he leaps from his mistress's arms, and amidst delighted shouts of "What a lark!"—"Dead, for a ducat!"—"Go it, old boy!" and other unsympathetic cries, rushes blindly across the platform, jumps off it headlong on to the line below, and remains there, dazed and helpless, evidently quite unconscious that the train is swiftly advancing to the spot whereon he stands.

The poor old lady's frenzy at this moment is terrible to witness.

"Oh, my Gyp, my darling—save him! save him! Watkins! Johnson! He'll be killed—let me pass—he'll be killed!" she shrieks wildly, trying to struggle through the live barrier of Etonians, who have all with one accord formed up in front to watch the progress of this tragic scene.

The white smoke of the train draws nearer, nearer; but neither maid nor footman, nor even the silent old gentleman who brings up the rear—presumably the husband of the frantic old lady—shows any heroic determination to rescue the unfortunate Gyp from the clutches of death.

Now the train is but sixty yards off. Gyp's fate is sealed.

"He's a gone coon!" shout the boys; when suddenly some one dashes on to the line, grips Gyp by the scruff of his neck, disregarding his yells and kicks, and almost as the buffers of the engine are upon him, swings himself back on to the platform.

The breathless silence which had fallen on every one for the six or seven seconds during which Gyp's deliverer was in jeopardy is now broken by a ringing cheer.   Again the air is full of shouts.

"Bravo, Treherne!"—"Well done, old boy!"—"Just like him—a regular Don Quixote!"

The hero of all these plaudits is one of the many Etonians.   He does not look particularly remarkable for anything but the placid contentment with things in general which characterizes most young men of six-teen when they have had a very excellent breakfast, and are looking forward to five weeks' entire immunity from brain-toil.

He bears Gyp, still struggling like a drowning rat, to the footman, whom he happens to see standing near him, and that functionary wisely transports him at once to the arms of his mistress.   The latter is so overcome with joy at his unlooked-for deliverance, that for a moment she has no thought for anything else.

Her husband, who has watched what has happened from a corner at the back of the crowd, where he was immovably wedged during the excitement, now comes forward.

"That was a very plucky thing to do," he says. "Maria, are you aware that the boy did that at the risk of his life?"

"Yes, so he did, the dear, brave fellow.   Where is he? I must thank him," answers the old lady, still stroking and soothing the ruffled Gyp.—" Johnson, go and find him ; I must thank him directly."

" Bring him to the carriage. We must get in, or we shall lose the train," says the husband, as he notes the scramble for seats which is going on amongst the high-hatted youths.

It is not without difficulty that the old couple do at last manage to secure two seats; for there is a strange unanimity about the boys who are already in the train. Whatever carriage the lady's-maid attempts to secure for her mistress and Gyp, a very polite and ceremonious boy gets up, and says, as he lifts his hat with elaborate courtesy, " I am so very sorry, but this carriage is engaged," or, " I beg your pardon, but those two seats are taken."

However, at last both the elderly travellers and the renowned Gyp are accommodated in an empty compartment—the only one left—and he is set free to roam round it at his own sweet will, the porters having discreetly shut their eyes and opened their hands as they closed the carriage door.

" Here comes Johnson with that brave young fellow. He doesn't want to come; he's trying to get off," says the old gentleman, whose head is out of the window.

Just then a porter rushes up, tears open the door— a large milliner's box, a bonnet-box, a dressing-bag, and a bundle of rugs in his hand.

Having deposited these articles on a seat, he says:

"Now then, make haste, miss, please. The train's just off;" and in scuffles a young lady.

Alas, alas! as she enters hurriedly, Gyp, whose nerves are still unstrung, takes the opportunity of effecting his escape from quarters he evidently finds depressing.

With an expression of triumph in eye and tail he runs airily up and down the platform, while the guard shuts the various carriage doors.

This is too much for the already much-tried old lady. She would positively have jumped out, and sacrificed herself and her husband, but that the relentless guard forbids her to move. As he stands there holding the door and expostulating, a scowl passes over his face.

"There's a boy got out, and is trying to catch the beastly dog," he mutters. "Well, he's lost the train, and serve him right."

It is too true. There are but three more doors to shut, and then the guard signs to the engine-driver, and jumps into his van as the train begins to move. But before it has actually left, as its speed becomes faster, a flushed face under a tall hat appears at the window, and a fat lump of black and tan descends suddenly on to the young lady's knee, much to her horror and surprise. She gives one little scream, and then cranes her head out of the window.

"He has got down," she says excitedly, "just in

time. In another moment the train would have been
going too quick. There he stands on the platform."

"Risked his life, and lost his train, and all for
a wretched lap-dog, belonging to an entire stranger.
And no one so much as knows his name. Well,
Maria, I hope you are satisfied with the events of the
journey so far." The speaker is the husband of Gyp's
mistress, and his voice and words betray that he is
not altogether pleased.

"O Ralph, Ralph," she answers, "I'm so frightened
—I mean grateful. Such a dear, darling boy! And
my sweet little doggie—what *should* I have done
if he had been killed? It was so noble, and I should
like so to thank him. And look, Ralph, how he
pants! I hope he'll get over it. But it was so dreadful, so very dreadful."

She goes on thus for some minutes, but as the rus-
tling of a newspaper, and the total eclipse of her husband behind it, tell her that Gyp is no longer in his
thoughts, after one glance at the young lady, whose
eyes are now fixed on the novel in her hand, Gyp's
agitated owner subsides into murmurs and whispers
over the stubbly coat of her beloved, while the train
speeds on its way to Paddington.

THE TREHERNE FAMILY.

I F any one asked Geraldine Treherne how many
brothers and sisters she had, that person was
certain instantly to regret the question; for Geraldine
was a great talker, and loved the sound of her own
voice better than almost anything else in the world.
She was ready to converse on every topic, and the
less she understood what she was talking about, the
more she seemed to enjoy airing her views. But once
start her on the subject of her own family, and she
was simply like a runaway horse—she could not be
stopped.

As she had five brothers and three sisters, and as
each of the four elder brothers went to a different
school, beginning with Geoffrey, the Etonian, you may
imagine that there was a good deal to be said, and so
Geraldine's unwary friends found.

Geoffrey, who considered it his especial mission to
crush Gerry on every possible occasion, was once in-
spired to make a riddle on the subject of his second
sister's flow of language. This was it—and you may

suppose how furious she was when she first heard it—
"Why is Geraldine Treherne like an over-full portmanteau? Because she will not shut up unless she
is sat upon."

The Treherne family lived in London. Mr. Treherne was a barrister with a very large practice, who
worked, as Geoffrey said, "like a nigger;" and well
he might, with so many boys and girls to provide
for. He was not much at home, and when he was,
he was too tired to enter much into the young
people's fun.

His wife, Lady Harriet, was gentleness and unselfishness personified; but her health was not strong,
and sometimes the high spirits of the children were
almost too much for her. She sat alone a good deal,
and though she had lived many years in London, she
went into society but little.

Whether she regretted the step she had taken in
marrying Claude Treherne against the wishes of her
parents—a step which had caused an estrangement
not even yet overcome—no one could tell. But she
generally wore an expression of patient resignation
which looked more like disappointment than fulfilled
hope.

Still, bitter though her thoughts were at times, she
loved her husband and her children with all her heart,
and her lonely hours were more often spent in making plans for their happiness and well-being than in

sorrowing over the old, long-enduring breach between herself and her parents.

There were days, however, when this subject would thrust itself forward, and the occasion on which I want to introduce you to the Treherne family was one of them.

She had been looking over some old letters—always a melancholy occupation—and among others she found the one which contained her mother's answer to the last appeal she had made for a reconciliation with her parents.   This is what it said:—

"MY DEAR HARRIET,—Your father is no better pleased with this last letter than with the others you have written.   He still says that 'you have chosen your own way, and that, rough or smooth, you must walk in it.'

"You do not say whether you are happy or not. but I earnestly trust that you are.   How I should like to see your little boy!   But why did you not call him after his grandfather?   Perhaps that would have pleased him, but I do not know.   He is very bitter about it all, and forbids me to do more than write this one letter.   I must send it off quickly, or he may insist on reading it.   Ever your affectionate mother,

"M. V. M.

"Harriet, Harriet! why did you do it?   I am so lonely now, and you were all I had.   Some day perhaps—"

There it ended. Lady Harriet gave a slight sob as she read the sad little postscript. Then she folded up the paper, now yellow and soft after its seventeen years of existence in her davenport, and returned it to its own drawer.

"Some day, perhaps," she murmured. "Mother, mother! I've waited a long time; how much longer, I wonder, must it be?"

She had hardly turned the key in the lock when a tremendous peal sounded at the front door. At the same moment, as though some electric force had been transmitted through the house, a stampede was heard in all directions. Doors were violently opened and banged to again; feet came tearing down the staircase, along the passages, and across the hall; and an excited hubbub of voices became audible. The only words to be distinguished were "Geoffrey," and "Come back;" but these were enough for Lady Harriet. The sadness passed from her face, and she opened the door and hastened down the stairs.

The hall was a scene of great excitement and bustle. Violet and Geraldine, Anthony and Leonard, with the three little ones, as their elders called them—namely, Joan, Gilbert, and Claude—were all surrounding Geoffrey, who stood in the vestibule, haranguing his cabman over his luggage, while the servants vainly endeavoured to get near enough to remove his portmanteau, hat-box, and other belongings from the door-mat.

"My young friend, my worthy young friend," Geoffrey was saying in his most elaborately patronizing voice (the cabman must have been at least double his age), "I have been this identical journey exactly eighteen times, and I have never paid more than the sum I have just given you. If you think I am a young man from the country, likely to be taken in by a voluble but wholly untruthful cabby, you are in error, or, as the vulgar have it, jolly well out of it."

"I ain't here to listen to a sermon. I wants my money, and what's more, I ain't goin' away without it," responded the driver of the four-wheeler, looking defiantly at his antagonist, and then glaring at the butler, who was advancing with a menacing expression.

Geoffrey looked round majestically. "Brown," he said, "take my things upstairs, please."

Brown and his assistant obeyed, and soon shouldered the luggage. "I must wish you good-night now," added Geoffrey to the cabman, stepping back and taking off his hat with great formality. "I hope you won't find it dull, or cold, or unprofitable, waiting here till my father comes back. He'll be here in about five minutes."

So saying, he shut the inner door and locked it, leaving the man gesticulating and talking with great vigour just outside. Needless to say, cabby, when he saw that his attempt to extort more than his due was a failure, ignominiously retired, banging the door violently behind him, and leaving Geoffrey master of the situation.

"How splendid, Geof!" cried his admiring sisters. "I'm so glad you beat him."

"Beat him! Did you think I was green enough to be done by a cabby at this time of day? I'm not quite such a duffer as that.—Hullo, mother! I didn't see you had come down. How are you? You don't look very fit. Come upstairs out of the draught. I wouldn't have kept the front door open so long if I'd seen you before."

So saying, he put his arm round his mother, and led the way upstairs, followed by the rest of the party, all talking at the top of their voices.

"Well, Gerry, your silvery tones haven't lost any of their power yet," observed Geoffrey as he consumed his tea in the morning-room. "I had cherished some faint hope that a slight weakness of throat would have come on while I was at home.—When is Gerry not quite so much of an ass as usual? Who can tell me that?"

"Oh, it's something perfectly idiotic, like that horrid portmanteau riddle," said Geraldine, really delighted, but pretending to be offended. Nothing Geoffrey did could be wrong in Gerry's eyes.

"Why, when she's a little hoarse, of course. Fancy not knowing that old thing!—By-the-by, I've made a

new friend. Guess who it is. You may have three
guesses each.—Claude, you begin."

"Animal, vegetable, or mineral?" asked that small
personage eagerly. He had but just begun to play
games with the big ones, and he was charmed with
this opportunity of showing how well he understood
them.

"Animal, of course, you little noodle," responded
Geoffrey amidst shouts of laughter.—"Now then, go
on, some one else."

"It's a man—a new Eton master," guessed Geraldine.

"It isn't anything of the sort, so there."

"It can't be an Eton boy, or you'd have known
him all through the half," observed Violet, who had
not spoken before. "Is it a lady?"

"Yes. Now guess her age."

"Five next birthday," ventured Claude, thinking
of his own mature years and his approaching natal
day.

"Wrong again. I didn't say a baby, Claude. I
said a *lady;* that means hundreds of times older
than you."

"Is she as old as Lady Desmond?" asked Leonard,
who had just reached Richard III. in Mrs. Markham.
"You know—

'She lived to the age of a hundred and ten,
    And died by a fall from a cherry-tree then.'"

"' What a frisky old girl!'" quoted Geoffrey. "No: my friend is a trifle ancient, but not quite as antique as that. How do you think I made friends with her?"

"Picked up her purse?"

"Wrong."

"Where did you meet her?"

"At the station."

"Perhaps you made room for her in your carriage when the train was very full," suggested Lady Harriet. "Shall I give you some more tea, dear?"

"No, thank you, mother; and your guess is wrong too. I made friends with her by throwing a hideous beast at her head."

"My dear boy, what *do* you mean?"

"It's true, mother, I assure you. No; this is what really happened. She, and her maid, and her footman, and her husband—but he went for nothing, a mere appendage not worth mentioning—arrived at the station, escorting the most horrid brute of a dog you ever saw. It did nothing but howl and yell and kick up a shindy. Just as the train was coming it got loose, and the old lady thought she had lost it, so I ran after it and fetched it back; and no sooner had she got with it into a carriage than the utter fool of a dog jumped out again. I wasn't going to have all my first trouble for nothing, so I collared it again and shied it in at the carriage window just as the

train was moving. And the beast of a guard wouldn't
let me get into his van, so I had to wait an hour and
a half before I could get off."

"O Geof, what a bore! Wasn't the old lady very,
very much obliged?"

"I'm sure I don't know. I heard her say she was
glad the dear little sweet darling hadn't been killed,
but I couldn't flatter myself that she meant me."

"Who was she, Geoffrey?" asked Violet.

"I don't know—Lady Something-or-other, the
flunkey said, but I didn't catch the name."

"Should you know her again if you met her?"

"I should know the dog, because it had a game
leg, and a white star on its forehead, and was the
most abject cur you ever saw."

"There's father; we must go. Come up to the
school-room, do, Geof, as soon as you've seen him,"
said Geraldine imploringly as a step was heard upon
the stairs.

In another moment the door had opened, and the
whole flock passed noiselessly out of it as their father,
clever-looking and care-worn, with the heavy footstep
of an overworked, overtired man, came in.

He seemed glad enough to see his boy, however,
and began questioning him about his place in the
school and his work for the last half. Geoffrey was a
very satisfactory son for an ambitious father. He had
plenty of brains, and lately he had begun to use them.

"I've been in the first hundred now for two halves, and there will be only three fellows between me and sixth form when I go back, so I hope I shall get in soon," he said.

"Have you been sent up for good this half?"

"Yes; I've had awfully good luck. I've been up five times. I can't imagine how it happened, but I think it must be because one day, quite by accident, I heard my tutor making a row about a window that was smashed in the hall, and I told him I'd done it. I wanted to get out early for a game at fives, and in unbolting the window my hand went through the glass."

"I don't see what that has to do with Latin verses," said Mr. Treherne.

"Only that he was up a tree, and didn't know what to do, when every one denied having anything to do with the window. He was so glad to be got out of the fix that he quite forgot to pitch into me, and out of gratitude he keeps sending me up for good to the Head."

"What rubbish, Geof!" replied his father. "I'm glad to say I have a better opinion of your tutor than you have."

"Oh, he's isn't half a bad fellow, only he is but human," said Geoffrey condescendingly, adding, "Well, I think I'll go up and get a little more refreshment in the school-room;" and he went away.

GEOFFREY'S OLD LADY.

"WHAT shall we do to-day?" asked Geraldine the next morning, as Geoffrey came lounging into the school-room with a yellow-backed volume in his hand.

"I am going to refresh my jaded brain with a little amusement," he answered. "But I don't want your chair, Gerry; I didn't mean that. Bodily, I am in a fairly prosperous condition; it is only my overwrought mind which must be relaxed."

"No; you can sit there, Geof. I had rather you did," said Gerry, who had vacated the one easy-chair the moment Geoffrey appeared, and now collapsed on to the rug. Her brother, muttering,

> "Take the goods the gods provide thee,
> Lovely Gerry sits beside me,"

sank into the big chair, settled his head on the cushion, put his feet on the mantlepiece, closed his eyes, and clasped his hands behind his head.

"Now," he said, "I am open to any reasonable offer for this afternoon."

" Well, then, Geof, I've got a most lovely plan. I've been looking at the map, and I see we could quite well go to the Monument, and the British Museum (I suppose we ought to go there, though I do think it is so dull), and the Tower, and St. Paul's, and the Whispering Gallery, in one day. To-morrow's Sunday ; but on Monday we can go to lots of nice things. There are nine picture-galleries in Bond Street alone, and there's the South Kensington Museum, and Madame Tussaud's, and the National Gallery, which really are not so very far apart. I don't mean that I haven't been to any of these places before, because I have, of course ; but it would be so nice to go again, without any one more grown-up than you."

" You're very kind, I'm sure," murmured Geoffrey ; but Gerry took no notice.

" Then we could say what we liked," she continued, " and stop just where we wanted to, instead of having to stay twenty minutes before a lot of stupid coins, and hurry on past the nice absolute stuffed animals, as we must when we go with father."

" Have you finished your discourse?" asked Geoffrey sleepily, as Geraldine stopped, panting with excitement. *Absolute* was quite enough like *obsolete* for her.

She nodded, and then glanced at Violet, who was sitting near the window, immersed in the " Pillars of the House," and did not seem to hear a word of what was going on.

"Then first, I would merely mention that an absolute stuffed animal is raving bosh, and that little girls shouldn't use words they don't understand and can't pronounce.   And secondly, I would suggest three amendments to your masterly scheme.   In the first place, I am perfectly certain that mother will not hear of our prancing about London by ourselves.   In the second place, I may observe—though, no doubt, that is a mere detail to a great intellect like yours— that to go to the Monument, British Museum, St. Paul's, and whatever the other thing is, would take till at least nine o'clock.   And thirdly, and lastly, that it would cost about £2 to go to all your Bond Street galleries and Madame Tussaud's."

"O Geoffrey, it wouldn't.   It wouldn't really."

"Yes, it would," said Violet, quietly closing her book and coming to the fire.   "Every picture-gallery is a shilling.   For three people to go to nine galleries would cost twenty-seven shillings.   Madame Tussaud's is one and sixpence with the Chamber of Horrors—that's four and sixpence ; and the South Kensington is a shilling ; and there are the cabs as well."

"Oh, well," said Geraldine, heaving a great sigh, "then we must give that up.   What else can you think of, Geof ? "

"I don't know.   I'm going to sleep—to dream—"

He gave a little snore, and Geraldine instantly

tried to tip up the rocking-chair backwards by a judicious shove.

"Ay, there's the rub," continued Geoffrey, without opening his eyes. "Leave me alone, and an inspiration will come."

Just then a voice was heard calling, "Miss Geraldine."

"Oh, bother! That's that horrid dressmaker. She always wants to try on dresses just when it's most inconvenient. But I suppose I must go," she grumbled, and she left the room.

"What a rum fish you are, Vi!" said Geoffrey, as soon as he and his eldest sister—only a year his junior—were left alone. "You never join in our jokes, and you never seem to be listening to us, and then all at once, like Madame La Farge in the 'Tale of Two Cities,' you turn out to have heard everything that went on."

"I despise mere talking for talking's sake," said Violet loftily. "But, Geoffrey, I have been thinking a great deal about the mystery, and I think I see through it."

"Mystery! there is no mystery. What on earth do you mean, Violet?" asked Geoffrey in amazement, opening his eyes.

"About your friend."

"My friend! What friend?"

"Why, the old lady you saw yesterday at the station."

" What of her ? "

" Why, who she is, and where she lives, and all about her. Don't you see how exciting it is, and how important for your future career ? "

" What unmitigated and unspeakable rot, Vi ! I never did hear—I really didn't think you were capable of such imbecility. As if the whole thing mattered one solitary farthing."

" It matters a great deal, and I shall make it my business to find out," said Violet oracularly. " I don't choose to be beaten by a thing like that."

" No : you always were the ferret of the family, poking your nose into everything, whether it concerned you or not," replied her brother. Violet was no favourite of his. " But you'll be beaten here, because there's nothing to go upon. Still, if it amuses you, why, poke away to your heart's content. *I* don't care."

" Some day you will be grateful to me—see if you're not," said Violet. " I know more about it than you think."

" Do you ? I wish you joy of your knowledge," said Geoffrey, closing his eyes again.

Violet said no more, and a few minutes later Geraldine, having apparently disposed very summarily of the dressmaker, re-entered the room.

" I've thought of the very place, Gerry," cried Geoffrey, " and I shall have much pleasure in taking you and Violet there this afternoon."

"Oh, what is it?" she asked eagerly; "because mother's got an idea too."

"It is to spend a few happy hours at the Deaf and Dumb Asylum, and see how much may be done by perseverance and industry, without the use of the human voice. I know you will be interested in that, Gerry, and I hope your family may be benefited in the future."

"Geof, you're perfectly horrid. No; what mother says is that she is going to see the old masters at Burlington House, and we may go too."

"What ecstasy of delight!" said Geoffrey. "It is a pity that I have just remembered a pressing engagement in another part of London."

"No; I know that's a make-up. But though you don't care for pictures, you really must come, Geof. You see, mother won't let us go about much alone with you. She says it doesn't look nice, though she has every conference—or something of that sort—in you. What a pity it is that Miss Newman has gone for her holidays already! We might all four have gone about together so nicely."

"That *would* have been rippin'," said Geoffrey. "What a picture! Miss Newman, with you and me holding on to her frock on each side, and Violet trotting just behind—all absorbing information at every pore. Why, I should have gone back to Eton quite a 'new man.'"

"Well, come to the old masters with us—do, Geof.
I told mother you would, and she'll be quite disappointed if you don't."

"If I must, I must," he answered, "but I've had
quite enough of the old masters at Eton. I didn't
expect to have them crammed down my throat the
moment I got home."

"Then that's settled. I'm so glad," concluded
Geraldine.—"Shall you come, Vi?"

"Yes, I shall come," she replied curtly.

"Vi? Oh, she'll go, you bet. She has a mission,
a vocation, and wherever I go there goes Violet, like
the albatross that hung round that poor beggar in the
poem,—eh, Vi?"

But Violet vouchsafed no answer.

Burlington House in the reign of the winter col-
lection is not quite the crush it is during the summer
exhibition. But it was crowded enough to fill the
uncultured soul of Geoffrey with wonder.

"What fun people can find in rambling round and
round a dozen rooms, staring at these smoky old
pictures, half of them mere black smudges you can't
see at all unless you screw yourself into some special
corner where the sun is, I can't imagine," he said,
as he followed his mother and sisters into Gallery IV.
"It's fifty times more of a joke to watch the people.
They *are* a rum lot, some of them. Hullo! if there
isn't—" He stopped short.

"Who, Geoffrey? What are you looking at? I'm sure that fat old lady is no one we know," cried Geraldine.

Geoffrey looked to see whether Violet was listening; but she was not, though she was a very little way off.

"Look here, Gerry: can you hold your tongue?"

"Yes, of course I can, Geof. Why do you ask me?"

"Because I don't want you to tell Violet. But there's my old lady—the one who has the imbecile dog with the game leg."

"Really? Oh, do let us go nearer. Which is she? Perhaps she will know you again."

"Don't be such a donkey, Gerry. I don't want her to know me, I tell you. Why should I?"

"I don't know, I'm sure; only it sounds like a sort of adventure. In a book, you would have to marry her, you know, Geof."

"What!—when she's already got a husband? O Gerry, you are too killing," said Geoffrey, going into such a fit of laughter that Violet turned round in astonishment.

"What is it?" she asked. "Gerry, what is Geoffrey laughing at so?"

"Nothing—at least, only something I said.—There she goes; look, Geof."

"There who goes?" inquired Violet eagerly, trying to follow Geraldine's glance.

"Only a beautiful being Geraldine and I were in raptures about," said Geoffrey. "Look! mother's going into the next room. What a mercy! Let's go after her."

"He has seen the old lady. I wonder which she is?" thought Violet. "I'm certain that's what it is, and I'm quite determined to find out what she is like and what her name is. Perhaps it's that lady in the long fur cloak. I shall go and see."

She crossed the room, and stood for a few seconds close to a tall, sallow-faced lady, who was looking at a dog of Vandyke's.

"Really he's wonderfully like poor Fido," she remarked to a friend who was standing by her.

Violet moved a little nearer.

"I hope Fido is better—I mean that he wasn't hurt yesterday," she said.

The lady turned round sharply, stared at the girl, then put on a double eye-glass, and stared again, Violet meanwhile growing redder and redder every moment.

"I beg your pardon," said the lady at last. "Did you speak to me?"

"Yes; I—I—said I hoped Fido wasn't much frightened yesterday. It was my brother who saved him from being lost at the station."

"I *think* you are mistaken. The animal I refer to has been dead for two years. And if I might venture to advise you, being a good deal older, I should say that it was better not to address total strangers in public exhibitions."

With this cutting observation she turned her back on Violet, leaving her rooted to the spot with shame and misery. Hot tears started to her eyes, but she tried to wink them away.

"How horrid, how *odious!*" she said half aloud. "I wish I hadn't spoken. But it was all for Geoffrey's good. I hate not being able to find things out. I suppose I oughtn't to have done it; but oh, she needn't have been so cruel!"

"*There* you are, Vi, are you? What on earth have you been doing, and what's the matter?" cried Geoffrey, suddenly coming to her side and peering into her face.

"Nothing," said Violet crossly. "But I'm tired. I hate this place. Where's mother?"

"In the next room. I'm with you as to hating these rotten pictures, but I don't see anything to cry about. I suppose you're tired. Come and sit down."

He took her to a seat in the next room, and before long her mother had finished her survey, and was ready to go home.

IV

VIOLET SUSPECTS SOMETHING.

"WHAT sort of day is it, I wonder?" said Geraldine the next morning as she fastened her frock. "I do hate a wet Sunday." She drew up the blind and peeped out. The sun was shining brightly in at the window as she threw it open, and she put out her head to inhale the fresh morning air.

"Why, there's Geoffrey running up the steps! Where *can* he have been at this time in the morning? What an extraordinary thing! I must go and tell Vi."

She opened the door of her sister's room, which led out of her own.

"Vi, isn't it odd—Geof has been out for a walk!"

"Nonsense, Geraldine. He wouldn't go out walking now. You know how he hates getting up early."

"I know that, but all the same I have just seen him run up the steps and come in at the front door. If you go down quick you'll meet him."

Geraldine did not mean Violet to act on her suggestion, which she had uttered only by way of showing how true her statement was. She was rather disconcerted, therefore, to see her sister run hastily off.

"Dear me! I wish I hadn't said anything about it," she thought. "Now perhaps Geoffrey will be angry."

Meanwhile, Violet had met her brother face to face, and instantly noted that his rather thoughtful expression changed to one of slight confusion when he saw her.

"Why, Geoffrey, where *have* you been?" she asked in accents of the most profound astonishment.

"What leads you to suppose that I have been anywhere?" he retorted.

"Geraldine saw you come in, so you see you can't pretend you haven't been out."

"I'm not pretending anything, except that I should like to go to my room, if you'll kindly let me pass," said Geoffrey in a voice which said as plainly as possible, "Shut up! and don't meddle with me."

Violet thought it best to give way, but she said to herself, "Another secret! But I'll find it out. I'm quite determined as to that."

At a few minutes before eleven the whole family started for morning service. The church the Trehernes went to was a very little way from their house.

Just as they reached the church door Geoffrey said,—

"Oh bother! I've left my prayer-book in my other pocket. I must go back, but I won't be five minutes."

He spoke to Geraldine, with whom he was walking behind the rest, and as he finished speaking he darted off homewards before she had time to answer.

"Where is Geoffrey?" asked his father a moment later, looking round.

"Gone back for his prayer-book. He'll be here directly," she replied; and they all went in.

They were too large a party for one pew, so Mr. Treherne and Lady Harriet sat in front with those of the little ones who were there, leaving Geraldine and Violet to sit in the seat behind.

As a rule both the girls tried hard to attend, and to profit by the service. It was not difficult to Violet to concentrate her attention, but the more volatile and younger Geraldine did sometimes find it an arduous task, and something happened to-day which quite distracted both the sisters at first.

Lady Harriet suddenly gave a start and whispered to her husband, who turned his head and looked at some one seated apparently some way off on his right. Then he spoke again to his wife. She seemed very much upset by whatever it was she saw, for she got out her pocket-handkerchief and began to cry, quite softly, so that no one could hear, only the two girls could not help seeing.

Geraldine came to the conclusion that her mother

was not well, and she bent forward to ask whether she would like to come out. But she shook her head.

It was quite a relief for once when the service came to an end, for Geraldine felt so anxious as to what could be the matter. " Are you better, mother dear ? " she asked, as they reached the door. ,

" Yes, thank you, darling. I saw a face I remembered, and it brought back old times—that was what it was."

" Whose face ? " inquired Violet.

" Some one's I love very much," replied her mother, and then she changed the subject. But Violet clung to it in her own mind.

" Is *that* a secret too ? " she thought. " Why, every one has secrets from me. It is too bad ; but I shall keep my ears open and find them out."

For the rest of the walk home she kept near her parents, so as to be within hearing of what they were saying.

At first they talked only to Leonard and Anthony, and then discussed the sermon, and spoke of another on the same subject they had heard somewhere else. But at last Violet caught the words,—

" They didn't see us, did they, Claude ? "

" No, I don't think so. I wonder where they are staying, and how long they have been in town ? Did you think them very much changed ? "

" She is—oh, terribly ; and I think he looks so

unhappy. O Claude, Claude! it makes my heart ache to remember how long they have kept up the old grudge. Think how many happy meetings we might have had during all these seventeen years."

"Yes; it is an extraordinary thing that they should bear malice for so long. We must still hope that some day they will see the uselessness of it, to say nothing worse." Just then he caught sight of Violet, who in her eagerness had come quite close, and showed by her face that she had been listening.

"Go and walk with Geraldine," he said with a displeased look; "and next time you see that your mother and I are talking about things which don't concern you, take pains to keep *out* of hearing."

Crushed and sullen, but not a quarter so much ashamed as many people would have been, Violet rejoined her sister, and found that Geoffrey, whom she had not seen since he ran back for his book, had caught her up and was walking with her.

"Where did you sit, Geoffrey?" she asked. But Geraldine answered much too quickly for him to be able to say a word.

"He sat at the back, but he says he could hear quite well, and see too. And as he came out he thinks he saw—"

Here she stopped short, and Violet thought it was in obedience to a warning nudge from Geoffrey.

"Thought he saw what?" she repeated.

But Geraldine only got crimson, and, wonderful to relate, kept silence. No one knew the effort it cost her.

Violet felt very angry, and would have said something to provoke a reply, only just then she saw that her father had rung the bell, and was about to enter the house.

She hung back, feeling injured and affronted, while the other six hastened in after him. Violet was in the act of mounting the steps slowly, when she heard a voice behind her, saying, " I beg pardon, miss."

She turned round, and saw a tall footman with a cockade, who touched his hat, repeating, "I beg pardon, miss, but will you be good enough to tell me the name of the young gentleman you've been walking with ? "

" It is my brother, Mr. Geoffrey Bentham Montgomery—" began Violet, with all the dignity she could assume. Then, with a sudden access of prudence, she drew up, saying, " But why do you want to know ? "

" My master, the Earl of Mannington, sent me to ask. Thank you, miss," answered the man, again touching his hat; and before she could gather her energies together sufficiently to ask the questions which came crowding to her lips, he had turned away.

" I can't run after him," she thought; " but what did he want to know for ? And who is the Earl of

Mannington ? It can't be Geoffrey's old lady, because she wouldn't be an earl. What can it all mean ? It is a mystery—another mystery ; and this time it is all my very own. I don't think I shall say anything about it. Geoffrey won't tell me his secrets, so I shan't tell him mine. I shall try and find out some more about it, and then, when I know, it will prove to them all that it is of no use trying to hide things from *me*."

She turned again towards the steps, but found that Brown had thought the whole party had come in, and had shut the door. So she had to ring the bell. Needless to say, the door was opened by Geoffrey.

"Did you want to see any one ? " he asked in a frigid voice ; "because the fam'ly is away—gone to Bournemouth for the winter, after a severe attack of scarlet fever. But I shall be happy to send a message. I am sorry not to ask you in, but my horders was very partic'lar not to admit strangers."

"Don't be so silly, Geoffrey," said Violet icily, stepping past him. "Really, one would think you were quite a baby, you are so very childish."

" Who is that very disagreeable young person, Geraldine ? Has she come for the under-housemaid's place ? Because if she has, tell her she won't do," said Geoffrey in a loud aside, as his sister went up-stairs.

Violet took no notice, but proceeded in offended

silence to her room.   Once there, she locked the door, and sat down by the window to think.

" It's my opinion," she said to herself, " that Geoffrey has not been to church at all.   There is something odd going on—of that I am certain.   And what is more, I don't believe I have been on a wrong track all this time.   Let me see.   First, Geoffrey wants to get out of that old lady's way, though he *says* he saved her dog from being lost.   Secondly, he went stealing out of the house this morning, no one knows why.   Thirdly, he made an excuse any one could see through, and wouldn't come to church with us. Fourthly, Lord Mannington has sent his footman to follow him—fancy that—actually to follow him, and find out what his name is.   I see it all now. Geoffrey is in some scrape ; he has offended Lady Mannington somehow.   She is the old lady he told us of—he said she was Lady Something—and so he wants to avoid her, and Lord Mannington too.   That is what it is.   How stupid of me not to see before ! Of course he went out early to ask the milkman, or some one of that sort, where he lived.   I suppose he had looked in the Directory, and couldn't find him there.   Perhaps he has only taken a house for the winter.   Then he must have seen him as we got near the church—I remember now there was a carriage at the door—and so he escaped.   But Lord Mannington must have caught sight of him, and now he knows

his name, and where he lives. No—oh, how lucky
that is!—he doesn't know his whole name, for I only
got as far as Montgomery. And as we've only been
in this house a few months, we're not in the Directory
yet. What a comfort! So, after all, I've been the
means of saving Geoffrey, though he wouldn't tell
me anything. I only hope Lord Mannington won't
call; but if he does, and he asks for Mr. Geoffrey
Montgomery, Brown will say he's not here. It will
be worse, though, if he writes; but I hope he won't.
Now I must make Gerry tell me all she can—that's
easy enough."

"Vi, Vi, what are you doing?" cried Geraldine's
voice at the door. "It's just luncheon-time. Do
make haste."

Thus adjured, Violet hastily flung off her hat and
jacket, and came out. Her face was flushed with excitement, although the unobservant Gerry did not
notice it.

"Father says he'll take us to the Abbey this afternoon," she said. "They're going to have 'Oh rest in
the Lord' as the anthem, and it'll be so delightful—
at least I think so. But Geoffrey doesn't want to come.
Isn't that odd? He doesn't like going to the pictures
either. How funny boys are!"

"And he didn't want to come to church, apparently," observed Violet, speaking as carelessly as she
could.

" Oh, it was only that he'd left his prayer-book at home ; he came afterwards.   He was in just in time for the *Venite,* he says."

" Did he say anything about the sermon ? " asked Violet warily, feeling that any ignorance displayed by her brother on that subject would be another link in her chain of evidence.

" I'm sure I don't remember.   I know I said I liked listening to Mr. Brownlow better than to the vicar, because I could understand him more ; and Geof said that the Eton sermons were so simple that all others seemed to him rather hard to follow."

" Did he follow the one to-day ? "

" I don't know—you can ask him.   But we really must go down.   There's the gong."

" Geof, could you follow the sermon ? " asked Geraldine as she caught him up in the hall.

" Yes.   Why ? "

" Only because Violet wondered."

" I'm sure it's very kind of dear Violet to take such an interest in me," said Geoffrey ironically.— " To what do I owe this anxiety, Vi ?   To my increased fascinations, or my evident need of improvement ? "

" Neither.   It's only Geraldine's nonsense," she replied, wishing with all her heart that she had not given her chattering sister such an opportunity.

" But Geoffrey never said a word to show that he

had really been at church, all the same," she reflected.

"Are you coming with us, Geoffrey, this afternoon?" asked Mr. Treherne at luncheon.

" No, father, unless you want me to look after Violet or Gerry."

" Oh no ; I can manage that. There will be no special crowd to-day."

" You might stay with me, Geoffrey dear. I should like to have a little chat with you," said Lady Harriet.

" All right—I will," he answered heartily, and so it was arranged.

V.

LORD MANNINGTON'S EFFORTS.

WHEN Monday morning arrived, Violet felt very nervous. With all her love of prying into secrets, and all her confidence that she alone could manage other people's affairs, she was not able to shake off a certain dread of what might happen to her if Lord Mannington did call, and by ill luck should be shown in.

" The worst of it is that he *may* be a friend of father's, and in that case even if Brown or Frederick did say that Mr. Montgomery wasn't here, he might ask for some one else, and then it would all come out," she thought.

It was a great relief to her when Geoffrey announced at breakfast that he was going to see if the water in Regent's Park would bear, as the frost had now lasted three days. By ten o'clock he had departed, and Violet could breathe freely.

Mr. Treherne had gone to his chambers, and as it happened, Lady Harriet, who seldom went out in the morning, had made an appointment for half-past eleven with a lady from whom she wanted the character of a servant.

Violet was alone in the school-room, which was on a landing between the drawing and dining rooms, at twelve o'clock, when she heard a loud ring at the door.

Her heart gave a great leap, and instinctively she ran out to discover who it could be. It was Frederick who opened the door.

"What a good thing!" thought Violet. "He's only been with us a week, so he isn't likely to know Geoffrey's Christian names."

Just then she heard a gentleman's voice say,—

"Is Mr. Geoffrey Montgomery at home?"

"No, sir. There is no one of that name here," replied Frederick.

"Surely I can't be mistaken in the house. The Mr. or Master Montgomery I mean is at Eton. He is about sixteen."

"There's only Mr. Geoffrey, and his name isn't Montgomery; it's Treean."

"Oh, really; then I fear I must have made a mistake. Thank you."

So saying, he went away, and Violet, who had been almost breathless with anxiety during the brief colloquy, heaved a sigh of intense relief.

"That's over; oh, how thankful I am," she murmured. "Well done, Frederick! I'm so glad you don't know how to pronounce our name yet."

Of course she said nothing about the visitor; and Frederick, who naturally attached no importance to the matter, said nothing either.

Still Violet felt that all danger was not over yet.

That afternoon she persuaded her mother to go for a walk in the park, which was close to the house. She did not want to drive, as she had taken out the carriage in the morning.

"You'll come too, *won't* you, Geof?" said Geraldine coaxingly. "We'll throw things into the Serpentine, and see how thick the ice is there. It'll be such fun."

"Oh, a tremendous lark. I know the sort of thing," rejoined Geoffrey—"toodling round and round that blessed park, nodding and grinning like a Chinese mandarin at every one who looks at you. It's not *my* notion of enjoyment, but I don't mind being a tame monkey in a string, for once."

"Do you mean you are coming with us?" asked Violet incredulously.

"Them was my sentiments," replied Geof. "Is it astonishment or pleasure which makes your eyes look like saucers at the idea?"

Violet did not answer, but in truth she was much surprised.

"He may meet Lord or Lady Mannington at any minute," she thought.

As usual, Geraldine and Geoffrey paired off together;

but when they reached the park Geoffrey insisted upon walking with his mother.

" You two good little things can trot along at the back," he said.

It was a bright but cold day, and most of the carriages were close ones. Suddenly Geraldine's wandering eyes saw some one making violent signs out of the window of a brougham.

" Look, Geof," she cried, " I believe that old lady wants to speak to you."

He looked round, and seeing the occupant of the carriage he took off his hat.

" She's stopping the coachman. There's the footman getting off the box. Why, he's coming this way."

" Oh, confound it all ! I can't stand this," said Geof, and he dived into the crowd of pedestrians, and disappeared before his mother had grasped what was happening.

" Never mind, Gerry ; look the other way, *do*," whispered Violet earnestly as the servant approached.

Instinctively she obeyed ; and the poor footman, who must have been rather tired of this fruitless search after a will-o'-the-wisp Etonian, went looking about now this way, now that—but all in vain. His thoughts being centred on " a young gentleman," he did not recognize Violet or even see her.

" What is it ? Where has Geoffrey gone to ?" asked Lady Harriet, quite bewildered.

"He saw some one he wanted to avoid, so he has run away to hide," said Violet crushingly.

"But why? Who was it?"

"You had better ask him," answered Violet.

"Vi, don't talk in that voice, as if it was anything wrong," said Gerry. "I expect it's only the old lady with the dog; and Geoffrey hates a fuss, and doesn't want a lot of speeches to be made to him of thanks and all that, and I'm sure I don't wonder."

No more was seen of Geoffrey until they got home. But when the two girls opened the school-room door, there he was, quietly seated by the fire, with the *St. James's Gazette* in his hand.

> "'She went to the cobbler's to buy him some shoes,
> And when she came back he was reading the news,'"

cried Geraldine. "Well, you *have* been quick, Geof! Was it your old lady with the dog that you bolted from so fast?"

"It was some one who dogs my footsteps in a way I don't like," he answered.

"No," thought Violet, "because you've done something wrong, and you're afraid of being punished.— What was that? I do believe it was the postman."

Without a word she swiftly left the room and flew downstairs.

Another moment, and she had the papers which had just been slipped into the letter-box in her hand.

"'Claude Treherne, Esq.;' 'C. Treherne, Esq.;' 'The Lady Harriet Treherne;' 'Miss Treherne'—oh, that's from Ethel Barnard. 'G. Montgomery, Esq.' There it is, and there's the coronet on the flap! Now, what shall I do with it? I can't give it to Geoffrey, because then it'll all come out about the footman, and the gentleman calling, and the scrape, whatever it is. What I really want to know is what he *has* done, and then I would go and get Lord Mannington to forgive him. I'm sure I could manage that. It would be something like Elizabeth walking from Siberia to St. Petersburg, to get the Emperor's pardon for her father, and every one says what a splendid thing that was to do. But then I can't know about it all unless I open the letter, and one mustn't read other people's letters. What shall I do? I think I'll just open the envelope to find out where Lord Mannington lives, and then I can go and see him."

Thus thinking, she began to tear the flap, when the school-room door above opened suddenly, and she had but just time to put down the other letters and escape into the dining-room with Geoffrey's one, which she hastened to put into her pocket.

To her dismay he came running downstairs and into the room.

"Hullo, Vi, what on earth are you doing here? Are you contemplating the frugal board? Or have you an irrepressible love for solitude?"

Violet was so confused in her reply, and got so crimson, that even the unsuspicious Geoffrey was surprised.

"Vi looks exactly as if she'd come to pocket the spoons," he thought; "what can she be up to?"

However, he said nothing more, but only went to the sideboard to extract a small corkscrew. "Gerry has produced a new bottle of eau-de-Cologne about as big as her head, and she wants the cork drawn," he explained, and then he went away, and Violet slowly followed him, feeling as if the letter in her pocket was red-hot, and was burning a great hole in it.

She found Geraldine in her room, taking off her out-door things, and it was quite impossible to obtain a moment for thought while that loquacious young lady was present.

"Isn't it like a book, Vi, this anxiety of the old lady's to thank Geoffrey?" she said as her sister came in. "*I* believe he really did something much grander and nobler than what he told us. He always hates to be thanked for what he does, and it would be just like him to do something splendid."

"Most people who have done anything splendid are not ashamed of it," observed Violet.

"Ashamed! he isn't ashamed. You don't understand Geof a bit, Violet."

"Don't I? I think you'll find I know more about him than a shallow little chatterer like you," retorted Violet, irritated beyond measure at such an assertion.

"I'm not a shallow little chatterer, Vi, and you're very cross and horrid. I can't think what's the matter with you. Geoffrey says you talk just like a blighted being in one of Miss Braddon's novels. You're not one really, are you?"

"That is not your business. I am a hungry being, at any rate, and I'm going down to tea this minute," replied Violet, feeling very angry, but resolved if possible not to show it. "Geoffrey doesn't deserve all I'm trying to do for him, that he doesn't," she said to herself. "But I shall not bear malice; I shall go on just the same."

As she came to this virtuous determination she felt quite a glow of pride at her own nobility and generosity.

She and Geraldine were generally such friends, different as were their interests and characters, that the door of communication between their two rooms was scarcely ever shut, and Violet had not another moment to herself until she went to bed that night.

VI

BROKEN DOWN.

WHEN Mr. Treherne came into the drawing-room that evening, he looked so white and strange that his wife started from her seat.

"Dearest Claude, what is the matter?" she asked. "You are worse, I can see. What is it?"

"I don't know; I've been feeling ill all day," he answered: "I suppose I am overdone. But the term is over now, so I can rest."

"You must see a doctor at once. You have never looked like this before. Do let me write at once and make an appointment with Sir Lewis ———."

She seated herself at the writing-table as she spoke. Her husband hesitated a moment; then, closing his eyes and sinking back on the sofa, he said, "Yes; I think perhaps that will be best. I feel to-night as I have never felt before."

He put his hand to his head with a gesture of exceeding pain, and said no more, even when Violet and Geraldine wished him good-night a few minutes later.

"I do hope you'll be better to-morrow, father," said the latter. "Isn't it a comfort that your holidays have begun ? "

All the way upstairs she continued to talk, and all the time she and Violet were brushing their hair. They were allowed a fire in one of the two rooms each night, and this evening it was Violet's turn for one, so Geraldine lingered on, still talking aimlessly about everything she could think of, until Violet became almost entirely silent.

"How stupid you are ! " at last exclaimed Geraldine with a yawn; "are you tired ? "

"Yes; I want to go to bed."

"I believe you mean to read a book by the fire, and that's why you don't want me to stay. I shall peep in in a few minutes and see."

"No indeed, I'm not going to do anything of the sort; I assure you I had not even thought of it," replied Violet so emphatically that Geraldine looked quite astonished. The fact was that Vi had just remembered that the key was on Gerry's side of the door, and so she could not lock her out.

At last even the "shallow chatterer" became sleepy, and went off to bed. Violet waited a few minutes until all was still in the next room, and then she got out the letter, which she had transferred to the pocket of her evening frock, now lying on a chair.

Geraldine had carried away the candle when Violet

assured her that she was not going to read a book, so she had to bend over the fire to see.

She could not help a feeling of shame coming upon her as she drew the letter out of its envelope.

"But I am only going to look at the address. I shall not read one word of the note; *that* would be most dishonourable," she said to herself.

Her eye had just caught the words, "98 Hyde Park Gardens," when the handle of the door—which Gerry, contrary to her usual custom, had shut—turned suddenly. Violet gave a tremendous start, and dropped the letter. It fell into the flame, and was consumed in a moment.

"Aha! Who was going to get into bed directly?" asked Geraldine's laughing voice. "And she *is* sitting up reading, after all. Is that Ethel Barnard's letter, Vi? You said you had heard from her. What does she say?"

"She doesn't say much; you shall read it to-morrow," answered Violet, hardly knowing what she said.

"Then what is that envelope? You haven't had two letters to-day, have you?"

"No; it's not mine at all—I mean it's not your business—it's nothing. There!" and she threw the envelope into the fire, watching the little blaze it made, with a bitter smile. "Now, you've done enough, I hope," she said to Geraldine. "*I'm* going to bed, if you are not."

"So am I, but I can't think why you won't tell me what that was," replied Gerry.

However, as Violet evidently did not mean to satisfy her, she thought it best to disappear into her own room.

Violet's reflections were not, as may be imagined, very pleasant ones.

Having taken a letter which was not hers, and destroyed it, although by accident, she felt very uncomfortable and very guilty. But like every one who has done wrong, and yet hopes to escape the evil consequences of the action, she kept making excuses for herself and finding palliating circumstances.

"I never meant to keep the letter, and I never meant to read it, and of course I didn't mean to burn it—that was entirely an accident. It is very dreadful; but what is to be done now?"

Conscience whispered, "Tell your mother the whole story, from beginning to end." But this was a suggestion so disagreeable and so humiliating that she would not listen to it for a moment. "No," she thought, "after all, there's no great harm done. If the letter hadn't been burnt, I don't know how I should have managed. I never thought of that. But of course I couldn't have given it to Geoffrey with the flap torn; and yet it would have been almost like stealing deliberately to keep back another person's letter. Now I'm only not giving it to him because I

can't; it doesn't exist any longer. No one knows that
it was written, except Lord Mannington, and he may
either think it was misdirected, or else, if it was to
request Geoffrey to go and see him on purpose to be
punished or scolded, he won't be surprised that he takes
no notice and doesn't go. No; 'silence is golden.' If
it was Gerry, she'd let every single thing out at once;
but I can hold my tongue, so I shall simply say nothing
whatever about it, and very likely it will still turn out
that I've saved Geoffrey from a scrape."

While Violet was thus endeavouring to justify herself by these hollow sophistries, a distressing scene
was going on in the drawing-room. For a long time
after the girls' departure, Mr. Treherne lay white and
quiet on the sofa in the stillness of physical exhaustion,
but with many thoughts and feelings busy in his brain.
A terrible, nameless fear, which for many a long day
had haunted him like the shadow of a sword suspended
over his head, now for the first time seemed to take
shape and form itself in his mind. Slowly but surely
a dread had seized him, a dread of coming mental
prostration, when the keen intellect upon which his all
depended, which was the instrument of his progress
and the basis of his hopes, should be paralyzed, and
when, with all his schemes shattered to the dust, he
should be compelled to live that life of inglorious ease
which with his whole nature he loathed and despised.

All his life he had been an ambitious man, an eager,

energetic, striving man. All his life he had been engaged in one long endeavour to cut and hew out his
onward way. From his first school scholarship to his
college fellowship, from the time he was called to the
bar till now, when he was a leader of acknowledged
fame, he had kept his eyes fixed upwards on the sum-
mits he hoped to gain. But the long toil, the rare
holiday, the fierce strain, had left their mark upon his
frame; over and over again for months past nature
had cried to him to pause and rest, and had cried in
vain. But even *his* stern energy and unbending will
were conquered now.

As he lay there, with that horrible sensation of
helpless languor, with that ceaseless throb, throb like
a mill-wheel turning in his head, he recognized at
last that the struggle was over and his defeat had
come.

Was his career, then, irretrievably blasted, his am-
bition fruitless, his future a blank? Inexpressibly
bitter was the thought. Next, ashamed of his egotism,
his ideas reverted to his family—to his wife and children. What to these would his overthrow imply?
Well for them indeed that his savings had not been
inconsiderable—that for years he had resolutely stored
up the full half of his professional income. But how
marred and maimed would be their lives! How little
should he be able to do for his sons and daughters of
what he had meant! And then, what if this approach-

ing illness should prove more even than prostration ? What if it should end in his death ?

Mr. Treherne was a brave man and a Christian, and the shudder that thought involuntarily caused was on their account, not on his own. Who would comfort his poor wife ? who would act a father's part to his little ones ? Some strong promptings of the heart, which he could not repress, made him break through the mist of pain which rendered all exertion hard, and speak.

" Geoffrey," he said faintly.

The boy looked up, startled, from his book.

" Geoffrey, come here."

Then, as he stood by the side of the sofa, Mr. Treherne stretched out his arm and took his son's hand.

" My boy," he said, " promise me that if the time should ever come when I am not able to take care of your mother and of your brothers and sisters, you will do your best to take my place. Will you promise me ? "

" O father, father !" cried Geoffrey, " what do you mean ? You are not so ill as all that, surely ? You are not going to—to—"

" To die," said his father. " No, Geoffrey, I hope not —I think not. God knows, though, what else may be in store for me—I cannot tell. But will you promise what I ask ? Will you promise, whatever may hap-

pen to me, to play your part like a man—to think of
them first and of yourself last, and to do all that is in
you to protect them and help them?   My boy, can you
promise it?"

"Yes, father," he answered huskily, "I do promise.
God help me to keep it."

"He will help you—I believe you will keep it,"
said his father, and then he relaxed his hold on the
lad's hand at last, and sank back, utterly spent.

Geoffrey's heart was very heavy as he mounted the
stairs to his room.   He reverenced his father; and
he loved him more than a casual observer of the
way the two behaved to one another would have
imagined.

Though rather cold in outward manner, Mr. Treherne was a man of strong affections, but he required
a nature of greater demonstrativeness than his own to
make the advances which he could not make himself.
Geoffrey's hearty cordiality and entire absence of self-
consciousness were very attractive to his father; besides which he was proud of his son, and had expected
a good deal from him in the future.   He thought he
had observed in Geoffrey traits of a finer character
than is often to be met with, and though he would
not perhaps have owned it, he even admired his boy
for the firm principles and manly straightforwardness
which he had shown on several occasions.

On the other hand, Geoffrey had a profound veneration for his father's abilities, and an awestruck admiration of his industry. He often heard his name spoken of as a leading barrister, and one who was sure of a seat on the bench—perhaps even of attaining a still higher eminence yet; and Geoffrey felt a thrill of pride when he heard these remarks, and often resolved that some day he too would work "like a nigger," and try to do something to fulfil the hopes which he somehow knew that his father secretly cherished on his behalf.

After Geoffrey had gone, Mr. Treherne lay for about half-an-hour silent and motionless, his wife watching him with speechless anxiety. Then he opened his eyes.

"Harriet," he said, "something tells me that my career is over. No, I don't mean that I am dying," for she had given a piteous cry at his words, and now came to sit on a low chair by his side; "I mean that paralysis or some other affection of the brain is coming on. I don't think I shall ever work at my profession again. Well, I must be thankful—I *am* thankful—for the success I have had. Ultimate fame is for the strongest, not only the cleverest, at the bar. But what grieves me is that in the event of my illness Geoffrey will have—" He put his hand again to his head and stopped confusedly.

"Dearest Claude, don't think any more to-night," entreated his wife. "Come to bed, and to-morrow we

will see Sir Lewis and learn the truth. I pray that
it may not be so bad as you think."

After a little more persuasion he let himself be carried off, Lady Harriet feeling as she left the drawing-
room that another burden was now added to her
already aching heart.

VII

SCHOOLROOM CONVERSATION.

GEOFFREY woke the next morning with a sense of impending disaster heavy upon him. For a few minutes he lay still in bed, thinking over his father's words, and recalling his look of prostration and helplessness.

Then he roused himself with a start.

"He has worked all these years for me," he said to himself, "and all the jolly times I've had I owe to him. Now I'll work for him, and, please God, I'll show that I'm not unworthy to be his son. But, O God, if it be thy will, don't let him die."

He was on his knees now, pouring out all his hopes and resolutions before Him who was to Geoffrey, little as a mere acquaintance would have guessed it, his one strength and stay, his counsellor and refuge every day—not only on Sundays, as is the case with some people—in each event, great or small, of his life. He had recently been confirmed, and in the vows he then made the bond between him and the "Friend that

sticketh closer than a brother" had been drawn still
more near together.

"How is father?" he asked as he entered the breakfast room.

"He has had very little sleep, and I am afraid he
is no better. I hope to hear this morning from Sir
Lewis that he can see him to-day. I am very anxious
about him," replied Lady Harriet, on whose countenance sleeplessness and distress had too plainly written
their tale.

The breakfast-time, generally so merry, passed
slowly. Every one felt that there was a shadow over
the house, and even Geraldine's chatter was silenced.

Violet was full of her own thoughts and her own
schemes for the general good. She was not without
feeling, and at any other time she would have sym-
pathized with her mother's grief, but just now she was
so completely absorbed in her plans about Geoffrey
and the letter, that she had little thought for other
things.

She was so absent and *distraite* all the morning,
that at last even Geoffrey's astonishment was roused.
The three young people were sitting in the schoolroom.
Geoffrey was engaged upon a book which, to judge by
his occasional bursts of laughter and muttered ejacula-
tions of "What an awful joke!" must have been of a
satisfactory nature. Geraldine was knitting a sock,
and making vain attempts to draw her companions

into conversation. Violet was apparently reading also, but her eyes wandered very often from the page before her, and her forehead continually contracted in a frown.

"Oh *dear*, how dull this is! I *wish* I had never promised to join that Odd Minute Society," said Gerry at last.

No answer.

"It's a great bore to have to do a certain amount of work every day—*isn't* it, Geof?"

"It's not quite so easy as doing a certain amount of talking. Why don't you join a society for doing that? You'd land every prize that ever was offered."

"Vi, have you ever seen Miss Manton? She's rather old, but you can't think what a nice dog she's got."

"A game leg," said Violet without looking up.

"*What?*" asked Geraldine in amazement.

"I mean she lives in Hyde Park Gardens; doesn't she?" answered Violet.

"In Hyde Park Gardens! What *are* you thinking about, Vi? You know quite well her house is in Cromwell Road, Kensington."

"Gerry," asked Vi suddenly, having apparently paid no heed to what had just passed, "what is mother going to do this afternoon?"

"Stay with father, I should think. Why?"

"Because if she doesn't want the carriage, perhaps she'll let you and me go out for a drive."

"O Vi, Vi! what fun!" cried Gerry, throwing down her knitting and jumping up excitedly. "We'll go and make calls; or shall we go to some big shop? That's what I should like best. I do love to walk out, with a great monster shopman just behind, and say, 'Please, put the parcels in the carriage;' and then Frederick comes up and takes them, and the man outside with the gold band on his hat opens the door, and there is such a nice little commotion. It makes me feel so deliciously grown-up. Let's do that. —And then, Geof, you'll come too, won't you?"

"Yes; and crawl after you while you buy one pocket - handkerchief here and three boot-buttons there. I think I see myself," said Geoffrey contemptuously. "If I did, though, *I* shouldn't let any monster shopmen follow me. I should just chuck the parcel into my pocket and walk off."

"Oh no, no; there'd be no fun in that. But I shall ask mother.—Where would you like to go, Vi?" asked Geraldine, aware that her ideas of happiness and her sister's were seldom identical.

"I want to go to Hyde Park Gardens—I mean Marshall and Snelgroves—or—or Madame Tussaud's," replied Violet in the most confused way, turning a brighter pink every moment as she saw what a slip she had made.

"You seem a little mixed. Pray, who is the friend you are so anxious to see in Hyde Park Gardens?" inquired Geoffrey.

"No one at all—at least hardly any one. I don't know why I said it; perhaps I saw it in my book," she answered hurriedly.

"Probably, as you're reading 'Ivanhoe.' It's just the sort of place that would be mentioned," said Geof, going back to his own volume.

What was it that so completely distracted Violet's thoughts from what was going on? It was a new idea which had quite suddenly come into her mind.

"Only suppose," she had thought, "that Lord Mannington should somehow find out about Geoffrey, and come to see him, or write again. Then it would all come out about my taking the first letter, and I should get into such a fearful scrape. Whatever happens, I *must* not let them meet now, for my own sake as well as Geof's. What I must try to manage is to see Lord Mannington myself, and tell him that I have brought my brother's apology, and I hope he will forgive all that has happened. Then I shall have saved Geof, and not have got into trouble myself."

It was at this point in her reflections that she made the suggestion about the carriage to Geraldine. The next thing was to arrange that she should be left alone in it. That was far more difficult to manage. Geoffrey steadily refused to join in what he gracefully described as "humbugging about in a stuffy old brougham."

So the two sisters started by themselves. Geraldine had a very important mission intrusted to her—the choice of a piece of stuff to make a frock and pelisse for the first baby of a former servant; so they drove to Marshall's first.

"How shall I manage to get off?" thought Violet, as she followed her sister into the shop.

Geraldine's air of importance, as she marched up the shop, was delightful to see. She might have been the delegate of some Oriental prince come to order furniture for an entire palace.

"I wish to see some frock-stuff—I mean dress material," she said, in a very stiff, "woodeny" voice.

"Gerry," said Violet, "shall you be very long?"

"No, not very. But you know, Vi, there is a good deal to be considered, and of course I must be all the more careful, as it is not for myself. There is mother to be thought of, as well as Sarah; and it is so difficult, because I know mother likes dark things, and Sarah's favourite colour is scarlet."

"Do you want anything else afterwards?"

"Yes—oh yes—at least, let me see."

She opened her purse, and counted its contents anxiously.

"Three and ninepence halfpenny," she said. "Yes; I shall want a good many other things."

"Then I think I will go and inquire at Mrs. Ravenscroft's—you know mother said we were to do that—and then I'll come back for you."

"O Violet, *don't*. There's no hurry, and I shan't really be very long. Here come the stuffs; do, *please*, help me."

"No, I can't. Remember, it's half-past four already; we had the carriage so late. Besides, Geof is quite right—the shop is dreadfully stuffy and hot. I don't feel well at all. I must get out into the air at once."

Gerry cast an imploring look at her. She could not own before the "monster shopman" that she did not like being left in that big place all by herself. But Violet took no notice of her beseeching glance. She walked quickly off, and Gerry's eyes filled with helpless tears, one of which, to her inexpressible shame, dropped on to the piece of serge she was examining.

VIII.

A DESPERATE EXPEDITION.

"MY business is much too important to be put off for Gerry's childish shyness," said Violet to herself, as she jumped into the brougham and told Frederick to go to Mrs. Ravenscroft's. As soon as she had made the proper inquiries there, she drove on to 98 Hyde Park Gardens. She felt very much excited as she drove along, and she was thinking so intently that she was quite surprised when the carriage stopped and Frederick appeared at the window.

"Ask whether—whether—Lord Man—no, Lady — no — Lord Mannington is at home," said Violet. "Oh dear, dear, how annoying to have stammered like that!" she added to herself. "But I hadn't thought about that part. I suppose it sounds rather odd for me to ask for a gentleman. And yet it is Lord Mannington I want to see."

"Yes, miss," said Frederick's voice as he let down the step.

Violet was so much ashamed of the way she had

hesitated, that she quite bolted into the house out of sight, and did not observe the row of carriages which stretched down the street, nor the knots of servants standing about on the pavement.

" Miss Treherne," she heard the footman say, and the words were repeated by several others as she mounted the stairs.

Sounds of music reached her from above, and a hubbub of many voices.

"Oh, how dreadful! how very, very dreadful ! There is a party going on," she thought. " Oh, what *shall* I do ? "

" Miss Treherne," announced the butler in an appallingly loud voice, which Violet thought must be heard to the furthest corner of the room, but which Lady Mannington, who was near the piano, did not, in fact, hear at all.

It was a large room into which Violet was shown, but large though it was, it was completely crowded with people. There was hardly room for her to get in at the door, and when she was once in, the guests who had made way for her closed up again, and she was wedged immovably in.

Which was her hostess, and whether her host was there, she had no means of knowing. She felt intensely uncomfortable, especially when she noted the surprise with which some of the gentlemen near the door watched her come, all alone, into such a large assembly. She looked round; not a single familiar face could she see.

" Oh that I had not come ! " was all that she could say to herself, as she squeezed as far out of sight as possible.

In a few minutes the piece of instrumental music came to an end, and the voices rose higher than ever. Some more people came, and as they were announced an old lady came forward to receive them. She was short and fat, but she did not look particularly good-natured, and Violet's heart sank within her more and more.

After a time some crimson curtains were drawn aside, and people began to stream into another room for tea and coffee. Violet was swept along too; and a kind old gentleman, seeing that she had no one to speak to, said,—

" Can I get you a cup of tea ? Or would you like coffee ? "

" Tea, please," she answered, relieved at the bare idea of having something to do besides staring at other people, and being stared at by them in return.

But, alas ! when the tea was handed to her past several ladies, who stood between her and the table, Violet, unused to such a crush, and not skilful in handing full tea-cups about, took it a little slanting, and the spoon fell out.

" Oh, I'm so sorry," she began, diving for it at

once, not seeing that a gentleman's elbow was almost touching her saucer. As she stooped, he gave a sudden turn, hit his arm against her, and down went tea-cup, saucer, and boiling tea. The china made such a clatter, that every one looked round, and the tea fell upon a lady's brown velvet dress. The wearer did not look pleased, and when she saw whose cup it was, she made no effort to soften her voice as she remarked to some one close by,—

" That comes of bringing school-girls about to this sort of thing. It is most ridiculous, and does neither them nor their elders any good."

She swept past Violet with great acerbity, and the latter felt as if to creep under the table would be a relief.

"I *can't* get out, however much I wish to," she thought. " I couldn't ask every one to make way for me. Oh, how I wish I could see Lord Mannington! Then I could say what I meant to, and ask him to let me go."

After a song had been sung, to which the ladies listened with evident reluctance, and the whispering gentlemen did not listen at all, the people really began to depart. Violet watched very carefully, and at last discovered a tall middle-aged gentleman standing by the curtains, who seemed to shake hands more often than any one else.

" That must be Lord Mannington," she thought,

"and he's saying good-bye to every one. Now, I'll try and make my way up to him."

She began to struggle through the people, and a long and difficult affair it was to reach her goal.

But at last she found herself close to the tall gentleman. She placed herself just in front of him, too anxious and nervous to reflect how odd she must look, and fixed an earnest gaze upon him. She was wondering how it would be best to open proceedings.

Before long his attention was drawn towards this basilisk-like young lady, standing so motionlessly before him. He wondered "what the little girl could want" (Violet was small for her fifteen years), "and why she kept staring so at him, and whom she could have come with, and whether—"

"Please," said Violet at this point, thinking she perceived a slight lull in the farewells, "can I speak to you for a moment?"

"Certainly," he replied courteously, bending his head down to listen, but looking a good deal surprised.

"If you wouldn't mind coming a little away from the people, out there"—indicating a recess where there was nothing but a white bust on a tall pedestal (the gentleman murmured, "'Far from the madding crowd;' how romantic!")—"or perhaps you would like to finish your good-byes first? I can wait, and what I want to say will take some time."

"Then we'll begin at once. Suppose you come with

me into the library; we shall be quite undisturbed there," he said, leading the way out of the room, while Violet reluctantly followed. "Now," he said, as he shut the door, pulled forward a chair, and poked up the fire, " let me hear. But perhaps I had better leave the door open. You mustn't let your people go away without you."

" I haven't any people with me; I came alone," replied Violet.

" Oh, I beg your pardon," said the gentleman, trying not to show how very extraordinary he found his visitor's statements.

She went on: " What I want to say is only that Geoffrey is very sorry for what he did the other day. He begs your pardon and Lady Mannington's, and he hopes you'll say no more about it."

The gentleman opened his eyes wider and wider as Violet uttered this carefully prepared and studiedly vague speech.

" Geoffrey!" he repeated as she ceased speaking— " Geoffrey! who is he? I have never heard of him. I have no clue whatever to what you mean. I am very sorry—it is my fault, no doubt—but would you mind explaining a little?"

" Why, last Friday, Geoffrey—that is my brother— was coming back from Eton, and he threw a dog at Lady Mannington's head, and we knew you were both angry."

"It does sound as if she might be a little annoyed. But I assure you she has not complained of it to me," he replied, biting his lips.

"No, because you knew all about it—you were there, you know—and you have called to see Geoffrey, and then you wrote, and you sent the man, and so did Lady Mannington. But, indeed, we're very sorry, and of course he won't do it again. So will you ask Lady Mannington to forgive him, and not try to punish Geoffrey any more?"

"Do you know, I think you must be under some mistake. You say I wrote to Geoffrey. What did I say in my letter?" asked Violet's *vis-à-vis* with rather a bewildered look.

"I don't know," she answered hesitatingly. "I—I—" Her confusion seemed to make him bolder.

"And how do you know it was Lady Mannington at whom he threw the dog?"

"Because—because—a footman told me so. He ran after me."

"A footman," he repeated in a voice of the most profound astonishment, "ran after you?"

"Yes, last Sunday," went on Violet.

"Did Geoffrey speak to him?"

"No; he didn't see him."

"Was it after he read the letter you say I wrote that he asked you to come here?"

"No," and Violet blushed crimson, and wished that the gas had not been turned up so high.

"But he must have read the letter. What did it say? Surely he must have told you, even if he didn't let you see it."

"No, no—oh, don't ask me any more," she cried, getting up hastily. "I can't tell you anything else. I only want you to promise that you won't say any more about it to anybody."

"Say any *more?* I think I can promise you that," he replied, noticing with still increasing surprise Violet's excited eyes and vehement, agitated manner.

"Thank you," she said. "And now I must go at once. It is so dreadfully late, and I've left Geraldine at Marshall and Snelgrove's all this time." She went up to shake hands. "I am very much obliged to you for forgiving Geoffrey," she added. "Good-bye."

"Good-bye," said the gentleman; "but pray let me see you to your carriage—or are you walking?" as an idea suddenly struck him.

"Oh no; the carriage is waiting—at least I hope so. I told it to."

"Well, as we have made one another's acquaintance, I hope you will tell me your name."

"My name is Violet Treherne," she answered promptly.

He had just asked, in a very much surprised voice, "Are you Claude Treherne's daughter?" when some one came hastily into the room, and seized his arm, saying,—

" Oh, *here* you are.   I say, Armadale, isn't this awkward ?"

He was obliged to turn to him, and Violet took the opportunity of slipping away.   Another minute, and she was in the carriage again.

" Where to, miss ?" asked Frederick, struggling to conceal his intense disgust at her lateness.   Lady Harriet almost always sent the carriage home if she was going to stay very long at a place.

" Marshall and Snelgrove's.   And be quick, please ; Miss Geraldine is waiting."

" It's no good going there, Miss Violet," said the gruff voice of the indignant coachman, Wilson ; " they shut at half-past six, and it's close upon seven now."

" Oh dear, is it really ?   How dreadful !   I had no idea I had stayed so long ; but I couldn't help it. Then you must go home, Wilson," announced Violet, adding to herself, as she sank back upon the seat,—

" *What* a scrape I shall get into !   What *can* Gerry have thought ?   Oh dear ! and when I had done the other so—so—not beautifully exactly, but without letting out anything.   What shall I say has kept me ? I mustn't tell a story, and yet I can't say just what did happen.   I must think about it."

And think she did until she came to her own door.

IX.

STRAIGHT TO THE MARK.

MEANWHILE a very different scene was being enacted in Mr. Treherne's study. Sir Lewis had come and gone. Alas! his verdict had confirmed his patient's presentiment. He had absolutely forbidden him to continue his head-work.

"If you go on," he said, "I will not answer for the consequences; I will not even say that they may not be fatal. You are in a most critical condition, and any trifling now would be highly dangerous. For six months, or perhaps a year, you must have entire mental rest."

"And then?"

"Wait till the time comes, and we shall see."

"But do you think I shall ever be able to resume my professional work, or are you hiding from me that I am a wreck—a mere useless hulk—for the rest of my days? I conjure you to tell me the truth."

"My dear sir, frankly, I cannot. The whole matter depends upon two things—your absolute obedience to my directions now, and the amount of recuperative power your constitution possesses. Do not lose hope —there is no reason for that. But, on the other hand, refrain from building too much on the future."

With that he went away.

"Dearest Claude, there is some hope, there is indeed," said his wife, when she heard the physician's dictum. "Do not despair. Many a man has tried perfect rest, and averted what seemed like an utter break-down. Why should not you?"

He lay silent on the sofa, and for some minutes made no answer. Then he said bitterly: "Harriet, when you talk like that you don't take in what all this means, as I do. It means loss of income, living on savings—it means retrenchment of every kind. It means being forgotten by the world—the legal world —as a dead man out of mind. But whatever it may bring to me, I am resolved on one thing: it shall not bring the ruin and downfall of all my hopes for Geoffrey."

"O Claude!" The words burst from Lady Harriet's lips involuntarily.

"No," he went on; "I will not allow it to be the utter collapse of Geoffrey's career—a boy who deserves to have every advantage, and who would make the most of every opportunity."

"If it were, dear, Geoffrey would see that it is unavoidable. He would understand that illness such as this is sent to us, and must be borne without repining," she answered, struggling even as she spoke to reach such a frame of mind herself.

He made no answer, but as he lay there before her she could see how his brain was working, by the flush on his forehead and the way in which the muscles of his face moved and contracted. This was not obeying Sir Lewis's orders.

"Claude," she said at last, "you know you are thinking and working just as much as if you were studying a brief. Do try and put the worries away; it is your only chance."

"I know," he said, opening his eyes. "But I must see Geoffrey and tell him everything. I cannot rest till then."

"Would you like to see him now? He is at home. Or would it be too much for you?"

"No; let him come, let him come. But oh, it is hard to tell him, or any one, that I am mastered—beaten—done for!"

A few minutes elapsed, and then Geoffrey came in very softly.

"How are you, father?" he said. "Mother told me you wanted to speak to me."

"Yes, so I do. Sit down there," answered Mr. Treherne, pointing to a chair opposite. The boy obeyed, a wondering, half-apprehensive look on his face.

There was a slight pause, then Mr. Treherne said,—

"My work is over, Geoffrey. From this day forward I am known no more at the bar. I have struggled against this month after month, hoped against hope, but now it is over."

Geoffrey uttered a sound which was almost a cry.

"No, it is not bodily death, only professional extinction," his father went on. "But if I fought against it any longer, paralysis of the brain would come on, and then either death or something still worse would ensue."

"O father, father! how cruel it seems!" broke from Geoffrey. "You, who have worked so hard, and that every one talked of as certain to be a judge at least. It does seem hard—unjust."

Such had been his own thought, but he had enough self-control not to own that to his boy. Besides, uttered aloud, it somehow sounded more rebellious, more guilty, than when it only surged through his own brain unspoken.

"The blow, Geoffrey, will fall on you all, as well as on me," he said. "I have been living on my professional income, and now that will cease. I shall be very much straitened for means."

He stopped, and Geoffrey's heart gave a great throb as the words fell on his ear. For a minute he could not speak.

"I see what father means," he said to himself: "he means I must leave Eton," and with that thought came the sudden collapse of all his dearest hopes and anticipations. His spirit seemed to die within him.

Leave Eton, without ever reaching sixth form, without being in the eleven, without getting into "Pop"—honours which the future had seemed reliably to promise; leave his friends—and Geoffrey had a great many; give up the last two years, which now seemed to him to be quite the best of his whole school-life!

In the midst of his reflections his eye fell on his father's prostrate form, on his clenched hands, on his keen, worn face, and sad, hopeless countenance.

"How different he looks from what he did!" he thought. "He has striven his utmost to give me all I've had, and now he's beaten, by no fault of his own. What is my little disappointment compared with his—the destruction of twenty years' toil? I am a selfish brute. I ought to make it easier for him, and I will." He roused himself, and turned towards the sofa. "I see what you mean, father. I am to leave Eton," he said. He stopped another moment, just for strength to speak calmly. "Well, of course it is very beastly, but it can't be helped. I am awfully sorry for you—of course it's much worse for you than for me. If I can do anything to make money, I'll promise you to work like the veriest galley-slave—I will indeed. And—and—I am so awfully sorry about you're being ill, father."

His voice failed, and he could say no more. Now the words were uttered, he realized what they had cost him, and how completely they had clinched his fate.

But every word he spoke fell like balm on Mr. Treherne's troubled mind. Proud of him before, he felt more proud than ever now. An old Etonian himself, he knew what the blow must be; he could appreciate the sacrifice which his son was thus unasked and uncomplainingly making.

"If I had suggested it," he thought, "it would be different, but I never even meant it. And now he proposes it. Shall I accept?"

"Geoffrey," he said at length, "you are offering me more than I had intended to ask. I had meant to keep you at Eton for another year, at all costs."

"Did you, father? Oh, thanks most awfully. But—but—why me in particular? If you are going to be so much worse off, why should I go on the same? I mustn't be the only one that won't suffer. No; I'd rather—at least, I mean I am quite ready to leave at once. I am, really, father."

"But I can't send you to the university, Geof. That will be impossible."

"Oh, of course; I know that. But can't you get me anything—a clerkship of some kind?" asked Geoffrey, keeping the hot tears out of his eyes by sheer force of will, and trying to speak in a composed, business-like tone.

"Yes, I daresay I could. But it is not positively necessary for you to begin to make money immediately. I don't mean that. Only the cost of keeping you at an expensive school would be a heavy drain upon me."

"I see." He thought a minute or two, and then continued: "Father, I've thought of something. I saw in the *Times* the other day that there is an Oxford scholarship at St. Nicholas—I forget what it is called—to be competed for at the end of this month. It isn't the usual time for scholarships, you know. Why shouldn't I have a shot at that? I'll grind away all day from now till then, and perhaps I *might* get it. It's £110 for four years."

"Is it? That is a very valuable scholarship. Well, you can try; but I don't think any one straight from school could get it on such short notice, and with no special preparation."

"But, father, I'll get a coach. I've got a tenner of my own—part of the twenty pounds Uncle Charley left me, you know. A coach for a month won't cost more than that."

"I meant special preparation at Eton."

"Oh no, I haven't had that. But I really did sap last half. How awfully lucky that is!"

"Yes; I got your report this morning, by-the-by, but I didn't read it, my head was too bad. Oh, here it is:—

" ' *Treherne.*—First-rate abilities. Has improved greatly in application. Greek prose excellent. Mathematics fair. Latin good and improving rapidly. Has worked well this half. General conduct excellent.'

" Come, Geof; you couldn't have done much better than that," said his father, his dull eyes brightening, and all his old energy seeming to revive. " You are a son worth having."

A deep crimson overspread Geoffrey's face and neck at these words.

It was to please his father that he had worked so hard last half. It had cost him an effort, but now he felt rewarded indeed. Being a boy, and an English one, of course he could not say what he felt.

" Well, I'll try for this thing then," he observed, " and even if I don't get it I shall be no worse off than I am now. Besides, I may find something else going. And after all, a clerk is not like a monk or a Jesuit,—he doesn't promise to go on for ever. A fellow might have a stroke of luck even if he did seem to be glued to a writing-desk."

But his father made no response. His temporary strength was gone now. He had been much excited by the conversation, and the reaction had set in. He was lying back in his old attitude of helpless prostration. Geoffrey glanced at him, and instantly ceased talking.

" I must call mother," he said; "all this planning and thinking have been too much for him."

Even as he uttered the words half aloud, the door opened, and his mother beckoned him out of the room.

" Geoffrey," she said, " I want you to go round to the stables, and see whether the carriage has come back. Frederick is not here, but still I cannot imagine why the brougham should still be out. Geraldine has just come home in a cab."

" In a cab, mother! Why, where is Vi?"

" She left Geraldine at Marshall and Snelgroves, saying that she was going to inquire after Mrs. Ravenscroft's father. She did not return; so after waiting a long time, Geraldine had to take a cab home. It was an extraordinary thing for Violet to do. I can't understand it at all."

" Then where can Vi be all this time?"

" I have no idea. Wilson may possibly have driven back to the stables, through some misunderstanding. That is why I want you to go and see if he is there."

Geoffrey went, but no tidings could be heard at the mews. Just as he got back, however, Violet drove up in the brougham. Her face was not promising; but, as usual, Geoffrey went straight to the point.

" What on earth have you been up to, Vi?" he

asked. "Gerry says you left her to kick her heels in a shop the whole afternoon, and she's had to come back on the top of a costermonger's cart."

"What nonsense!" ejaculated Violet, marching up the steps with an air of immense disdain, but with much inward perturbation. Her pulses beat faster than ever when she encountered her mother, looking very grave, at the top of the first flight of stairs.

"Come in here, Violet," she said, opening the school-room door; and Vi was obliged to follow.

"Violet, where have you been since you left Geraldine?"

"I went to Mrs. Ravenscroft's, mother, and asked after old Colonel Sandys. He got much better, and he's gone away. There was a party going on—and I got jammed into the drawing-room, and couldn't get out."

"The drawing-room! But why did you go in? I only meant you to leave my card, and then come away."

"Frederick opened the door, and—and—I didn't think—at least I forgot about Gerry," said Violet, who had to choose every word in order that she might achieve her double object of satisfying her conscience and deceiving her mother; for she had by this time brought herself to think that if she did not utter a falsehood in so many words, "it would do."

"But when you saw that there was a party,"

persisted her mother, "you must have known I should not wish you to go in."

"Yes; but I didn't notice that there was one until I was half-way up the staircase—I didn't really," she rejoined eagerly, relieved to be on true ground at last.

"But the question still remains—*Why* did you leave Geraldine alone? There was no hurry about Mrs. Ravenscroft."

"Gerry was so slow, and I got so tired, and the shop was so hot, and—and—"

She could think of nothing more to say, but even to herself her excuses sounded lame and insufficient.

"You have acted very wrongly, Violet," her mother said. "As the eldest of the two, you were in charge, and you had no right to leave Geraldine all alone. I have great anxieties just now, and I hoped you would have helped me to bear them. But if you only consult your own inclinations and impulses, I shall not be able to depend upon you for any assistance. I am disappointed in you, Violet."

If it had been Geoffrey or Geraldine, they would have said they were sorry, but Violet made no reply at all. She only waited a moment, to see whether her mother was going to say any more, and then left the room, with an expression in which resentment and triumph were strangely mingled.

Lady Harriet sighed deeply. It was a great trial

to her that her eldest daughter had lately grown so self-contained and unsympathetic.

"She might be such a comfort to me, if she only would," she thought. "Perhaps it is my fault; I don't know. I must be patient and gentle with her. Who knows—she may alter yet." .

X.

SENT TO COVENTRY.

GEOFFREY rose in what he considered the middle of the next night—that is to say, he got up at six o'clock in the morning, and by seven he had drawn up an elaborate scheme of work for himself, which with characteristic energy he began to put into practice at once.

He had had no opportunity of telling Gerry of his new plans the night before, and she was very anxious to know why he had got up so early. At breakfast —Mr. Treherne not being there—she attacked him boldly.

" I heard you go down, Geof, but I couldn't believe it was you; only then you came up again and dropped a book outside my door, and I knew the house-maids wouldn't be carrying books about. Is it your holiday task you want to get over, so as to have it off your mind ? "

" No, it isn't. I'll tell you presently, if you can keep quiet long enough for me to speak," he answered.

She would have retorted, but just then Lady Harriet

rose from her chair, breakfast being over, and Geoffrey got up to open the door for her. At that moment Brown appeared, to ask if Wilson could speak to his master.

"No," said Lady Harriet; "Mr. Treherne is still very unwell. But I will see him if he will come into the hall."

"He's come to ask if I wouldn't like a gallop on old Marmion; what a brick!" ejaculated Geoffrey.

"No; it's to say that the tabby kitten we gave him is lost—I know that's it," said Geraldine in a mournful voice.

As they spoke, Violet, looking very odd and flushed, tried to force her way upstairs past her brother and sister.

"Hullo, Vi, where are you off to so fast?" cried Geoffrey. "Have you got another little expedition on hand, or is there a secret waiting for you upstairs you're afraid of missing? I'll tell you another, if that one's gone."

"Be quiet—let me go," she said irritably, and she wrenched herself free from his detaining arm and disappeared.

"Good-morning, Wilson," said Lady Harriet. "There is nothing the matter, I hope?"

"Yes, my lady, I'm sorry to say. Marmion has caught a chill, and he's very bad to-day—very bad indeed. I had to go for the 'vet' first thing this morning."

"Dear, how unfortunate!" said Lady Harriet, while Geoffrey gave a little whistle of dismay. "How did it happen, Wilson?"

"'Twas last night, my lady, waitin' about so long in the row outside Lord Mannington's. We couldn't move about, you see, till the other carriages drove off; and a nasty fog came on—enough to give any Christian his death of cold, let alone a delicate 'orse like that."

At the recollection of the two hours' waiting Wilson gave an injured little cough behind his hand.

Lady Harriet was so utterly overwhelmed at his words that she could scarcely speak, but she managed to say,—

"I am very sorry; it will be an additional worry for Mr. Treherne. But you can only do your best under the veterinary's directions. We must drive one horse in the carriage to-day."

"Very good, my lady. I'll do all whatever I can, and let you know how the 'orse is to-morrow."

So saying, he put his hand to his forehead, and departed down the kitchen stairs.

"Lord Mannington!" exclaimed Geoffrey; "what on earth can he mean? Why, Violet pretended she had been at Mrs. Ravenscroft's all the time. And Lord Mannington's of all people! Hullo, mother! what's the matter?"

He rushed forward, for she had almost fallen. Fatigue, sleeplessness, anxiety, had already done a good deal, but this proof of deliberate deceit in Violet was a greater blow than all.

"I am only a little faint," she said; "I shall soon be better."

She rested a few minutes, and then went up to her husband, while Geof and Geraldine joined Violet in the school-room. She was sitting by the window, apparently absorbed in a book.

She looked up anxiously as they came in, and then down quickly, as though she would not have them notice her agitation.

"Violet," said Geoffrey, standing in front of her, and looking as neither of his sisters had seen him look before, "were you at Mrs. Ravenscroft's the whole of yesterday afternoon?"

"It is no business of yours—you have no right to ask," replied Violet, without raising her eyes from her book.

"I have no necessity, you mean, for it has all come out. You were at Lord Mannington's for two hours, and Marmion will probably die of the cold he has caught."

Violet started, quite put off her guard.

"Oh dear, how unlucky!" she exclaimed. "I wish I'd sent the carriage back, and taken a cab myself."

"What did you go to Lord Mannington's for? I insist on your telling me, Violet," continued Geoffrey, taking her book away and forcing her to look at him.

"I went to apologize for you, Geoffrey, as you might have guessed," she answered proudly; "and much gratitude I get for it."

"To apologize for me! You've either gone off your head, Violet, or else this is another little invention, like the one about Mrs. Ravenscroft."

He turned to his other sister, who was observing Geof's ebullition of wrath with wide-open, terrified eyes. "Now look here, Geraldine: I am extremely sorry and deeply ashamed to find out that one of my sisters is a li—, does not speak the truth."

"Geoffrey!" almost screamed Violet, starting from her chair.

"Does not speak the truth," repeated Geoffrey unmoved.—"And I forbid you, Gerry, to talk to her until she has confessed to mother everything she has done and said, and got her forgiveness. Do you hear?"

"Yes, Geof.—But O Vi, *do* go and say it all at once. It is so dreadfully wicked to tell stories, and —and I *can't* not talk to you, I really can't."

"You must, Gerry. If you don't, I shall think you like deceit and hypocrisy, and I shall send you to 'Coventry' too. So there. Mind, you are upon your honour not to speak when I am out of the room."

"Very well, Geof; I will try," said poor Gerry, to whom this threatened punishment was so terrible that she would have done anything to escape it.

"As for you," added her brother to Violet, with studied coldness, "the sooner you wipe off this disgrace, the better for every one—for yourself, for Geraldine, and for the credit of your family. You've done more mischief by your meddling this time than you can probably ever repair. But as you don't understand it, it's not my business to tell you."

So saying, he walked away, leaving Violet standing by the fire, the picture of sullen shame and offended dignity.

"O Vi, Vi! what does it all mean?" began Geraldine, and then she stopped short.

There was a moment's pause.

"Can't you go and—" began Gerry again, and once more pulled herself up.

"This is too miserable! I can't stay if I mustn't speak," she said to herself. "It's very odd, but I seem to have more than ever to say to Vi this morning. I shall have to go and sit in my bedroom. How cold it will be!"

She moved towards the door, but Violet stopped her.

"You needn't go," she said. "I shall not remain here any longer. I am not accustomed to hearing such language as Geoffrey used, and I do not mean to hear it again."

She swept proudly away; but the majesty of her exit was somewhat marred by her catching her dress on the door handle, and being jerked so violently that she tumbled down. Her frock gave way, and a great rent appeared.

"O Vi, I'm so sorry! Shall I mend it? Here's my—oh, I forgot again, but I suppose I may point," cried Geraldine, with great excitement and sympathy.

She raised her hand and pointed to her work-box. But every necessary for mending a tear was absent.

"Where is the thimble?" demanded Violet.

"In the—" began Gerry, and then stopped, and again pointed with her finger to the window-sill.

"Scissors?" demanded Violet.

Gerry wheeled round like an automaton on a stand, and silently indicated the top of the piano. But Violet thought she meant a book-case, and searched for them in vain, looking crosser every moment.

"I *wish* I might tell her. How my arm does ache!" thought Gerry, as she kept it up like a sign-post.

At last Violet discovered the scissors, and began her work. But in her confusion she did it all wrong, joining two sides which were not meant to join, and making an unwearable bundle of the drapery of the dress. Geraldine's feelings may better be imagined than described, as she watched her. Six times her mouth opened, and a sentence was begun. Then she remembered her orders, and closed her lips with a mighty effort.

The rent mended at last, or rather cobbled together

in a very peculiar way, Violet again took her departure, with what dignity she could.

But once outside the school-room, all her grandeur
melted away. She burst into tears, and rushed upstairs to lock herself into her own room.

"It is a cruel shame," she moaned. "I did it all
for Geoffrey's good, and now he turns upon me. And
if I told mother how I found out where Lord Mannington lived, she'd turn upon me too. Oh, how
miserable I am, and how unjust they all are!"

At that moment there was a knock at the door,
and Lady Harriet's voice said,—

"Violet, are you there? I want to speak to you."

Thus constrained, she reluctantly opened the door.
Her mother came in, and sat down by the bed, on
which Violet, red-eyed but defiant, had placed herself.

Lady Harriet did not exactly know how to begin.
She waited a minute before she spoke, and then
said,—

"Violet, Wilson tells me that you spent two hours
yesterday at the house of Lord Mannington. Is that
true?"

"Yes."

"Then why did you say that you had been at Mrs.
Ravenscroft's all the time?"

"I didn't say so. I said I had been to Mrs.
Ravenscroft's and inquired after Colonel Sandys; and
so I had. And then I said there was a party going

on; and so there was, but—but—it was at Lord Mannington's."

"Did you mean me to understand that the party
was at Lady Mannington's?"

Violet hung her head down and said nothing.

"What is a falsehood, Violet? Is it merely *saying*
what is not true?"

She made no answer.

"You know very well that it may be speaking,
acting, or keeping silence. The essence of falsehood
is an intention to deceive. *How* it is done is of no
consequence. Your conduct in this matter is a very
deep grief to me, Violet. But I cannot understand
anything of what has happened. Why did you go
to Lord Mannington's at all? It was a most extraordinary thing to do."

"I wanted to get Geoffrey out of a scrape."

"Geoffrey!—out of a scrape!" echoed her mother,
turning a shade paler even than she had been before.
"Do explain what you mean, Violet."

"I found out that the old lady at whose head
Geoffrey had thrown the dog was Lady Mannington,"
said Violet, who had so often said this to herself that
now she really believed it; "so, as I knew that Geoffrey
was very much afraid of meeting her, I thought I
would go and say he was very sorry, and would she
forgive him."

"Did Geoffrey know what you meant to do?"

"No."

"Does he know now?"

"No—not exactly."

"He would be justly angry that you should have taken upon yourself such an office, without his knowledge and consent. I shall ask him whether he has, as you imagine, got into any difficulty; but I cannot believe it."

"Oh no—please don't, mother."

"I shall certainly do so, for many reasons. But in any case, your going alone to Lady Mannington's on such an errand was most improper. You do not understand how wrong it was, nor how painful the idea of it is to me. But if your father were well enough to be told of what you have done, he would be extremely annoyed and ashamed. When he is better I shall consult with him as to what steps he thinks had better be taken to undo the mischief, if it can be undone."

"But what mischief? I can't think what you all mean. I've simply got Geoffrey out of a scrape, and he sends me to Coventry for it [O Violet!], and *you* talk of my having done mischief. I think it is very hard indeed."

She tried to look and speak like an injured martyr, but in reality Lady Harriet's words and extreme concern had startled her considerably.

"You have shown a want of modesty and a love of

self-obtrusion which Lady Mannington may well be shocked at," continued her mother.

" Lady Mannington did not even see me, or at least she didn't notice me."

" Then whom *did* you speak to ? "

" To Lord Mannington. I went with him into his library. He is very tall—over six feet high, I should think. But he shook hands at the end, and asked my name," announced Violet in a tone of great complacency.

" You certainly have been a simpleton, Violet, as well as a forward, meddling child," said her mother, with a nearer approach to anger than the girl had ever seen her display. " You cannot have seen Lord Mannington at all. He is a very small, slight man."

Violet looked and felt most dreadfully foolish. But she would not show it; she would make one more effort.

" Are you sure that you know him, mother ? " she asked ; " because who else *could* it have been ? "

" That I cannot say ; but I think you will hardly dispute my statement, since I am speaking of my own father."

" *Mother !* " cried the girl, springing to her feet in the vehemence of her astonishment.

But Lady Harriet could not stand any more. She had not meant to tell Violet what it was which made her conduct so additionally distressing, and now she had uttered the words, the old misery seemed to break out again with redoubled force. She gave a sob, which was almost a cry, and hurried from the room.

XI.

PUZZLED.

I F Violet could have peeped into Lady Mannington's boudoir on the evening of the party, she
would have heard a conversation which would have
rather lowered her satisfaction in the success of her
negotiation.

Gyp, overfed and snappish as ever, sat on the sofa
in his own particular corner, and his mistress, rather
tired after her exertions, sat by him, trying to keep
sufficiently awake to listen to what a niece who was
staying with her was saying.

Presently the door opened, and her husband and
Mr. Harry Armadale, her only brother, entered the
room. The latter seated himself on the sofa, not
observing the presence of the truculent Gyp, who
sprang up with an ominous growl, and made a gallant
attempt to bite his arm through his coat-sleeve.

Mr. Armadale was one of the most good-natured of
men, but this was a little too much. He rolled up a
newspaper which was lying near, and gave Gyp such
a smart tap over the head, that after one reproachful

glance at his mistress he slank away under the sofa, where he remained sulking for the rest of the evening.

"I hope you didn't hurt the poor darling, Harry," said Lady Mannington anxiously. She had submitted to the punishment of her beloved with infinite reluctance.

"Hurt him? No; if he had a few more hints of that kind, he would be less universally objectionable. Besides, I wanted to get rid of him that I might talk to you."

As he spoke he once more sat down by her, glancing as he did so at Lord Mannington, who had got out the chess-board, and was about to embark on a game with his niece.

"Maria," said Mr. Armadale, speaking in a subdued voice, "have you ever heard anything of Harriet's children?"

"No; only I know by the *Times* when there is another born. But do take care, Harry," she added apprehensively, looking towards her husband. "You know he never allows the subject to be mentioned."

"I know, but he isn't listening, and I must tell you this. But first I want to know, are there any daughters?"

"Yes; three. The eldest must be about fifteen."

"There is a boy, isn't there?"

"Yes; Geoffrey is his name. Why do you ask?"

"Only because of something very odd that happened to-day. A very young, young lady arrived all by herself a little before the tea and coffee began, and stationed herself by the door. She evidently did not know a creature; she did not utter one syllable, but remained motionless, like the offended spirit of some guest you had omitted to ask, until the tea began. Then she revenged herself for being dull by taking a cup of coffee and throwing it all over Lady Maxwell's velvet dress, with what result to that particularly placid and amiable being's temper you may imagine. As soon as people began to go, she edged her way up to me, stood just in front for about five minutes, with such a stony stare fixed upon me that I became quite nervous, and finally asked me to go away from the crowd, as she wished for some private conversation."

"Harry, she must have been mad! Most likely she was some harmless lunatic, who had escaped from her attendant."

"So I began to think. But imagine my feelings when she began an incoherent story about a boy named Geoffrey, and his being very sorry that Lord Mannington was so angry, and would he forgive him."

"What could she have meant?"

"I don't know, and I don't believe she did either. The more questions I asked, the more confused and frantic she looked. I really didn't like her going away by herself, but she said her carriage was waiting, and some one came to speak to me just then, so that my attention was distracted."

"But who was she? Did you find that out?"

"Yes—that is just the point. She said her name was Violet Treherne."

"And her brother is Geoffrey? O Harry, she must be poor, dear Harriet's eldest girl, and I never even spoke to her! What is she like?"

"Oh, she is nice-looking enough for a little school-girl—rather particularly so—until she speaks. But then she looks most extraordinary. She hesitates, and stammers, and blushes, and talks the most incoherent rubbish."

"How very shocking! Do you think really that her brain is affected?"

"I don't know, I'm sure; but I should think Treherne's must be, to let her go about alone to people's houses in that way."

"Did she know this was her grandfather's?"

"No, I don't think so. She certainly didn't know Mannington by sight, for she took me for him, and it didn't seem worth while to explain who I was. Indeed, she was so certain she was right about everything, that it would have been quite useless. Besides, it didn't strike me who she could be until she had gone."

"*Don't* say anything to Ralph about it, Harry. It is my one hope to bring him and Harriet together

again some day, and it is dreadful—most dreadful—
to find that there is anything wrong in one of her
children. Are you quite sure the name was Treherne ? "

" What name ? " asked Lord Mannington's voice
just behind, and they both started.

" Only a little girl—very nice-looking—that Harry
was telling me he had seen," said Lady Mannington
hurriedly, with all her usual nervous manner. " Her
name is Treherne, Ralph dear."

" Oh, indeed," he answered coldly, moving away.

" Eastover wants me to go and see him," announced
Geoffrey at luncheon, the same day that Wilson had
revealed Violet's escapade. " I shall have time this
afternoon, without interfering with my working-time.
He has sprained his ankle, and he wants cheerful
companionship."

" You'll have to sit up and make jokes, Geof.
What shall you begin with ? " asked Geraldine. " I
can tell you such a good riddle, if you like."

" No, thank you. Eastover has got a little beyond
riddles," said Geoffrey with great disdain.

" Then I'll tell you what, Geof. I've thought of
something really funny and amusing," continued Gerry,
quite uncrushed. " Go into the room on all fours, like
the man in *Punch*. Only mind you go to the right
house. You know he went to the next door, and

there was a party, and when he crawled in people thought it rather odd. But I suppose you're sure of the number, so you won't go wrong. It really would be very funny, Geof. I'm certain it would make poor Somebody—I forget his name—laugh."

"I think it highly probable; but as he would be laughing at me for being such a fool, your suggestion doesn't strike me as particularly happy, Gerry."

At half-past two he started off. It was a lovely winter afternoon, bright and inspiriting; and as he walked briskly along the pavement, his thoughts turned naturally towards his approaching examination and his chances of success.

"I'll work as hard as I can," he said to himself; "but all the same I've got such a short time that I mustn't count on winning. Still, even if I don't, father will be pleased that I've tried, and that's what I want most. The question is—if I fail, what ought I to do next?"

As he thus soliloquized, he turned a corner, and came suddenly upon a hansom cab which had just drawn up, and from which a small, elderly gentleman of dignified bearing was in the act of emerging.

He put his hand into his pocket, and withdrew it with an expression of dismay.

"Good gracious!" he exclaimed, "my purse has been stolen. How very annoying!"

"It *is* a trifle inconvenient," observed the cabman

insolently. "But I've know'd it 'appen to my fares before this, and it don't always prevent 'em from payin' in the end. You'll be good enough to give me my money just the same. 'Arf a crown, if you please."

The gentleman drew himself up.

"There is no necessity for being impertinent," he said: "if you will drive me to my house in Hyde Park Gardens, I will pay you there."

"Yes, that *is* likely. I ain't quite such a flat as that," rejoined the cabman, a puffy, coarse-looking man, who had evidently been drinking.

Geoffrey had involuntarily lingered to see the end of the little drama he had thus accidentally stumbled upon, and now seeing the gentleman's embarrassment, he stepped forward and took off his hat.

"I beg your pardon," he said, "but here is my purse. If it will be of any use, please take what you want, and satisfy this cheeky beggar."

The gentleman started slightly as he turned round and saw the lad standing there holding out his purse, with a slight flush on his eager young face.

"You are very kind," he said. "If you will give me your name and address, I will do as you suggest, and send you back the money."

So saying, he took the purse, and turned to pay the cabman.

As he did so Geof walked off, and by the time the gentleman had finished listening to the cabman's voluble explanations of why he asked half-a-crown for a shilling fare, the boy was out of sight.

"What an odd thing," he said to himself, "not just to wait one minute! I wish he had, for I'm sure he is some one I have seen before. I know his face perfectly, only I can't recall his name. I see there was only that one half-crown in the purse. I suppose he knew that. But two-and-sixpence is two-and-sixpence to a school-boy—at least it was in my time. What a good-natured fellow! I hope I shall see him again."

Meanwhile Geoffrey, who was in a great hurry, posted along towards his friend's house at the rate of about five miles an hour, thinking excitedly over his late adventure.

"Why, it was Lord Mannington himself. Oh, how funny! Fancy meeting one's own grandfather, and his not knowing you. It wasn't for me, though, to tell him who I was, and scrape acquaintance. But I'm awfully glad I was able to help him, as he's mother's father. She'll be pleased, I think. I should like most tremendously to help her to make it up with him, but I suppose it isn't my business. Anyhow I shan't do anything unless I'm quite sure she'd like it."

XII

A DEJECTED YOUTH.

THIS turned out to be a particularly opportune day for Geoffrey's visit to Eastover. He found him lying by the drawing-room fire, looking the picture of discontent and martyrdom, but he cheered up for a moment when. Geoffrey came in.

"Awfully good of you to come and look me up, Treherne," he said. " I've been glued to this confounded sofa now for a whole week, without a soul to speak to, or a thing to do to make me forget my disgusting sprain."

"Why didn't you let me know before ?" asked Geoffrey; " I hadn't an idea that you were seedy till your note came this morning. I'm awfully sorry, and especially that you've been alone all the time. It's hard lines that your people should be away. Where are they ?"

"Oh, *they've* been here all the time. They're only away to-day—gone to the wedding of a cousin who has to go to India next month," replied Eastover, as if *they* did not count at all. " But except them,

I've seen no one.   I haven't got any brothers, you know."

"Nor sisters, have you?" asked Geof, thinking how glad he should have been of Gerry's good-natured helpfulness and gay chatter, under similar circumstances.

"Oh yes, I've got plenty of *them*; they're at the wedding too," responded Eastover, in the same grudging voice.   Geof saw that the subject of relations was not a congenial one.

"And they must be duffers not to have given him anything to amuse him," he thought.

He glanced round the large, luxuriously-furnished room.

"You don't care for books, I suppose?" he observed.

"Oh yes, I do, when there's anything worth reading; but there isn't."

"What are all these things, then?" inquired the visitor, gazing on an enormous mass of paper-covered books which almost hid the floor all round the sofa. His eye caught a few of the names—*Punch's Almanac; Routledge's Annual;* Christmas number of the *Graphic; Judy Almanac;* Christmas number of the *Illustrated London News; Fun Almanac; Hood's Comic Annual; All the Year Round,* special number; *Truth,* Christmas number; *Belgravia,* Christmas number; *World,* Christmas number; "The Dark Abyss, or the Mystery Unveiled;" "A Deed of Dolour, or Sir Leopold's Last Leap;" "Murder will out, a Tale of Blood."

"Well, Eastover," cried Geoffrey, "I don't know what you call 'nothing to read.' One would think this was Ingalton Drake's, at Eton."

Eastover looked disparagingly at the Christmas literature.

"Oh, that trash!" he said; "I don't call those *books*."

Geoffrey felt inclined to ask what else they were, but he only answered—

"Well, what other kind of thing do you like? We've got lots of books. If you'll tell me of something you haven't read, I'll send it or bring it to-morrow, if we've got it."

"Thanks. But I don't know. I've read most things worth reading." (Geoffrey wished *he* had.) "Still, if you'd got a book I began once and couldn't finish—it was about a wretched little counter-jumper, who had a lot of money left him, and tried to improve his looks by dyeing his hair. It was a failure, and came out in no end of different colours, just when the people he wanted to impress went to see him."

"Oh, I know: you mean 'Ten Thousand a Year.' Yes, we've got that; you shall have it."

"Thanks," repeated Eastover languidly. "Is it very long?"

"Yes; it's a thundering sort of book, that'll last you all the rest of the time you're ill, I should think."

"Is it? Then I don't think I should care for it. I'm not up to anything that wants thinking about or remembering."

He heaved a deep sigh.

Geoffrey began to feel rather nonplussed. He was wondering what he could do for the enlivenment of the dejected Etonian, when something reminded him of the riddles which, in spite of his cool reception of her offer, Gerry had supplied him with before he came away.

"By-the-by, Eastover," he said, "I've got two Eton riddles for you."

"Have you?" was the reply. "I hate riddles; but they're better than nothing. Let's have them."

"Why are the collegers and oppidans like a corps of engineers?"

"Haven't a notion. But you ought to say oppidans and collegers—not collegers and oppidans."

"No, you oughtn't, and if you did you'd spoil the riddle," contradicted Geoffrey. "And they are like engineers, because they're all either sappers or minors."

But Eastover was one of those irritating people who never see a riddle till it is taken to pieces and explained, and by the time the meaning of *minors* and *miners* had been drummed into his head, Geof felt that he had had enough of riddles. But apparently Eastover had not.

" I thought you said you knew two," he observed. " That one was stupid. Let's have the other."

" When is a leg of mutton like the best school in the world ?" asked Geoffrey rather apprehensively, adding hastily, " But it's no better than the other. I don't suppose you'll see it."

" Well, tell us the answer, and I shall know."

" When it's eaten—Eton—don't you see ?" he said explainingly.

" Of course I see ; I'm not quite an idiot. It's better than the other, but I don't think much of it."

There was another pause. Geoffrey was again racking his brains to think of something to say, when the door opened, and a small boy came in.

" Oh, bother !" exclaimed Eastover crossly, " there's that little nuisance again. He's a cousin of mine who's staying here, and he's the worst specimen of a spoiled child you ever saw—a regular caution.—Come here, Frank, and speak to Treherne."

Frank advanced rather sulkily. He had heard most of his relative's speech of introduction, and naturally felt that it did him shameful injustice. What spoiled child ever considers himself such ?

Geof looked at the young man—he appeared to be about eight years old—with the experienced eye of one who himself possessed the luxury of a younger brother, and could see such a being's " points" at once.

Frank was pale and delicate-looking, with heavy eyelids, and a somewhat sleepy air. But there was a wicked twinkle in the corner of his eyes which showed the knowing Geoffrey that mischief was at present the principal end and object of the " little nuisance's" life.

" I suppose you came in to cheer up Eastover, old boy," said Geof, as he shook hands. " But you see I'm here instead, so you can go and amuse yourself."

Frank looked decidedly relieved, and hastened to depart before Eastover should give any contrary and less welcome injunction.

" That's a mercy," said the invalid, as the door was shut with a resounding bang. " Now tell me the news, if there is any."

For the third time Geoffrey ransacked his memory to think of something interesting to relate, but in vain.

" I haven't seen any of the fellows yet," he said, " since the holidays began, and I don't suppose I shall, I shall be sapping so hard."

" Sapping ? what on earth for ? "

" Well, you know, my father's been taken ill, and now he has to give up his practice at the bar. So I can't go back to Eton, and I'm going to have a shy at a scholarship at Oxford."

" Oh, I say, Treherne, how disgusting ! I'm awfully sorry. There are no end of larks coming off next half ; and you'd soon have been in sixth form, you're such a swell at your work. And you'd have had a splendid chance for the eleven, too."

"I know," said poor Geof with a sigh, "it's all a confounded nuisance, but it can't be helped. I must hope for luck at the scholarship 'exam,' that's all."

Eastover was silent. He was of a restless, energetic temperament: but though his enforced idleness, added to all the petting and commiseration he had lately received, had made him peevish and irritable, he was not really selfish or bad-hearted ; and the contrast between his own luxurious position—for his father was a very wealthy man—and Geoffrey's changed prospects filled him with pity, and with admiration of the way in which he bore his trouble : for Eastover knew what giving up the last two years at Eton meant. No one spoke for some moments. Geoffrey was the first to break the silence.

"So you see I'm not much good at news," he said. "If you'd like a sketch of a Greek play, or an abridgment of the Annals of Tacitus, I'm your man; but I'm afraid you'd hardly consider either much of a lark."

"No, I certainly shouldn't," said Eastover. "But I see I've been a brute all this time to think such a lot of being dull, when I might have had something so much worse happen. The doctor says if I stay quiet I shall be all right by the end of the holidays."

"I'm glad of that," said Geoffrey heartily ; and then the conversation strayed to Eton topics, Eastover growing much more cheerful under the influence of Geoffrey's cordiality and good-humour.

No subject more painful to Geoffrey could have been chosen, but he said to himself,—

"Never mind; I've come to amuse Eastover, and I ought to talk about whatever he likes best. If he enjoys talking of Eton better than anything else, I *should* be an ass to say that was the one thing I didn't want to do."

So he resigned himself to fate, and for the next hour discussed all the chances of success which certain distinguished fives-players, cricketers, and football-players had for the coming two halves.

At last the clock on the mantlepiece chimed half-past four, and Geoffrey got up to go. "Good-bye, old chap," he said; "I hope you'll soon be better."

"Good-bye," responded the other. "Come again soon, Treherne, there's a good fellow; won't you?"

"Yes, I will really;" and he departed, glad that on the whole the visit had not been a failure. Indeed Eastover looked a great deal brighter and better for the hour of school gossip which had cost Geoffrey such an effort.

XIII

"*HE'D SEEN HIS DUTY A DEAD-SURE THING.*"

O F course Eastover had forgotten to ring the bell when his visitor went away, so Geoffrey had to let himself out. He was on the point of closing the front door behind him, when he heard a piercing shriek, followed by an exclamation of horror in a man's voice. At the same moment Frank came rushing out of the dining-room, screaming with agony and fright, and holding out a ghastly little hand with three of the fingers chopped asunder at the second joint. They were hanging by a mere shred of skin, and streaming with blood. After him rushed a young footman, roaring almost as loud as the child.

Frank was, of course, quite frenzied with pain and terror. He tore past Geoffrey, and turned to go up the stairs, while the footman shouted wildly to him to come to the kitchen to see Mrs. Marsley.

I have not mentioned a peculiarity of Geoffrey's yet, as it has not been necessary, but now I am going to do so. I am sure no sensible person will despise him for it, especially as his conduct at Windsor Station showed that he was no craven who feared danger to himself. No, Geoffrey did not fear danger—he was certainly not a coward in the common sense of the word; but he was constitutionally nervous in some special ways. He dreaded and shrank from the sight of blood, and would have gone a long distance to avoid seeing any sort of wound or hurt. This characteristic was instinctive—inherent. He could no more help it than he could help having a fine appetite or a good temper. Many, or rather most, boys do not mind such things the least, but they made Geoffrey almost ill. He had witnessed several accidents in the playing-fields at Eton, and had always felt unspeakably thankful that there had been no need for his assistance. The first look at a bleeding wound made him feel sick and faint, and quite unnerved him. He had lately been revaccinated with some other Etonians, and the moment the doctor had touched the first boy Geof had fainted away, much to his companions' astonishment. Such being his natural temperament, it will be readily understood that his first impulse on seeing poor little Frank's condition was to rush away at once. And so it was. With a sickening thrill of horror he banged the door and ran down the steps.

But he had no sooner thus obeyed his inclination than he was filled with remorse and scorn at himself.

"Only last half I went through the ambulance lectures," he reflected rapidly; " and there's that poor little chap left to the mercy of a pack of screaming women and that howling flunky, who had quite lost his wits, I could see. Of course I should have stayed, and tried to do what I could. As usual, I am doing what I like instead of what I ought. But I *won't;* I'll go back."

He turned round, retraced the few steps he had gone, and then, remembering that he could not get in at the front entrance without ringing, he ran down the area steps and entered at the back door.

Voices and cries, and above all the yells of unlucky Frank, guided him to where he was, and the sight which met his gaze made him almost reel. There stood the child, in the middle of the house-keeper's room, surrounded by women, still holding out his streaming hand, his face as white as a sheet, and in front of him a large newspaper spread on the ground, which was momentarily becoming a mere pool of crimson.

Geoffrey made a huge effort to battle against the dizziness which came over him as he looked. Action he felt would be best, both for himself and Frank.

" Haven't you done anything for him ? " he asked, advancing quickly.

One of the maids turned round and sobbed out, " No, sir, not yet. We've sent for the doctor."

" And Mrs. Marsley, she's gone for a little vinegar," said another, " which we thought that might do him good, the poor mite."

"Or a little hot water to soak his hand in. Don't you think that might ease him, sir?"

"No," almost shouted Geoffrey; "and you'll drive him *mad* with pain if you give him vinegar. Get me three bits of stick, and I'll put the fingers straight on some splints. And it's *cold* water, not hot, he must have. Hot water would make the bleeding ten times worse."

"Yes, sir," said every one at once, and they began running hither and thither for water and sticks in a way that drove Geoffrey nearly frantic, since he did not know where to look himself for what he wanted, and so was obliged to wait. However, Mrs. Marsley arrived with the vinegar, and on being told Geoffrey's views she soon got him cold water. He plunged in the wounded hand, and just then James the footman reappeared. He was little more than a boy himself, and was still sobbing with fright, having been a witness of the accident; but he wished to do all he could, and he now came running in with three walking-sticks, which he presented to Geoffrey.

"Here's some sticks, sir," he said exultingly.

"Not *that* sort, you ass," replied Geoffrey, almost beside himself with exasperation. "Can't you cut me three little bits that'll fit his fingers, flat on one side?"

"Here's a bundle of fagots, sir," cried a kitchen-maid, bursting breathlessly into the room. Geoffrey pulled out his pocket-knife, cut the string, and began paring down a piece of wood as fast as he could.

"You do the same, and be quick about it," he said to the others; and they meekly obeyed. Now that he saw the state to which poor Frank would have been reduced without his assistance, he felt most thankful that he had come back. By this time his pity and his eagerness to do all that was possible had quite got the better of his repugnance to his task, and his hand hardly trembled as he took the little fellow's tiny fingers and placed them and the loosened nails in their proper position on the splints. Then he got out his handkerchief, and tore it into strips to wind round each finger. The cold water had made his work a little less difficult, but of course the bleeding was still very profuse, and Frank's groans were dreadful to hear. He had left off shrieking, and he let Geoffrey do all he wanted, until the latter said at last, as he wound some cotton round the linen binding,—

"Well done, Frank. You're a jolly plucky little chap."

After that Frank tried all the more to stifle his cries, but he kept moaning,—

"Oh, it does ache; it does ache."

"Go up and tell Mr. Eastover what has happened— he must have heard the screaming," said Geoffrey— "and say it's all right now till the doctor comes."

James, who was better by this time, departed to deliver the message, and Geof turned again to his patient.

"Look here, Frank," he said : "don't think I mean to hurt you more, but I must tie a handkerchief round your wrist, to stop the bleeding; and I shall have to pull it awfully tight, or it won't be any good."

Frank agreed, and got out his own handkerchief, which Geoffrey proceeded to tie. But when he began to make a tourniquet with one of the bits of wood, and to really tighten the knot, Frank's shrieks broke out afresh.

"I can't bear it—I can't; you'll squeeze me to bits," he yelled.

"No, I shan't. It's all right. It *must* be tight. See, it isn't bleeding so much even now," said Geoffrey, as he gave a final twist to his work, in spite of Frank's struggles and remonstrances.

"Now, keep your arm up, and wait for the doctor," said he, when his labour was over. "Here,—lie down on this sofa, and I'll make a rest for your arm."

Frank obeyed, and Geoffrey, assisted by the maids, pulled a little table close to it, placed a cushion on it, and propped up the wounded arm so that it should be above the heart.

He had just finished these arrangements when a bell rang loudly.

"'Tis the front door; that's the doctor," cried Mrs.

Marsley, who since her suggestion about the vinegar had taken a subordinate part in the proceedings.

James was close to the front door, and in another minute the doctor had come down.

He had no sooner entered the room and walked up to Frank's sofa than he heard a dull "thud" behind him, and turning round he saw Geoffrey lying prostrate on the floor in a dead faint.

"Poor young gentleman! it's been too much for him, and no wonder!" said Mrs. Marsley compassionately.

"What is the matter? Has he been ill?" asked the doctor, bending over Geoffrey's prostrate form.

" 'Tis the 'orror of it all," observed the kitchen-maid, "which he did everythink, sir, just like a doctor."

"It give me such a turn as I don't believe I shall be able to swallow another morsel to-day," observed another spectator.

The doctor took no notice of these remarks, but gave his attention to Geoffrey, who was speedily restored to consciousness. He felt very much ashamed of himself as he recognized Dr. Judson, who happened to be the Trehernes' medical man.

"Oh, do go and look after Frank," he said. "I'm awfully sorry to have been such a duffer. The fact is, I hate wounds and things of that sort—I always have. But I was all right as long as there was something to do which had to be done at once. It was when it was over I seemed to be quite done for; I don't know why. But do help Frank, Dr. Judson; he wants it much more. I hope you won't think I've made a mess of it by meddling; but I thought I'd better do what I could."

The doctor turned his attention to Frank, and when he had rebandaged the fingers with the lint he had brought, he said to Geoffrey,—

" You've done capitally, my boy. I never saw better amateur bandaging; and I think, as I see your natural repugnance to such things, that you're a fine fellow to have fought against it as you must have done. You are not staying here, I suppose ? "

" Oh no; I had only come in to see Eastover. I must be going now."

" Then I advise you to send for a cab; you're not up to the walk," said the doctor. " And if this hand gets perfectly right again, as I hope it will, it will be almost as much your doing as mine."

Geoffrey felt that Dr. Judson's opinion as to his powers of walking at that moment were true enough, so he despatched James for a hansom, and very soon arrived at his own abode, where, as he had no more money, Brown paid the fare.

He felt strangely tired and feeble. The fact was that the trial to his nerves had been great, and the strong restraint he had put upon himself began to tell now that the time of reaction had come.

XIV.

GEOFFREY'S EXPLANATION.

AFTER partaking of five cups of school-room tea and a proportionate amount of edibles, Geoffrey announced that he felt as "fit as a fiddle"— an expression which seemed perfectly clear in its meaning to Gerry. Violet, who was in a very majestic and unconversational mood, retired to the dignified quiet and dulness of her own apartment after tea, and then Geoffrey (openly rejoicing that the "wet blanket had hooked it") gave a graphic account of his afternoon's adventures, to which Gerry listened with entranced delight. Her comments, which were very numerous, were of so complimentary a nature, that had they proceeded from any one else they might have turned Geoffrey's head; but he knew too well what the hero-worshipping tendency of her mind was to be the least elated by her eulogistic remarks.

He had just reached the end of the story when Lady Harriet opened the door.

"Geoffrey dear," she said, "will you come with me

into the drawing-room ? I want to talk to you about something."

He assented, and followed her at once, wondering what could be coming.

" Geoffrey," she began, flushing uneasily as she shut the door and motioned him to a seat, " I know you will tell me the whole truth if I ask you about this story of Violet's. What was it that really took place about Lady Mannington's dog ; and how have you offended her and Lord Mannington ? "

" Offended them, mother ! Why, I haven't offended them—at least, as far as I know. This is exactly what happened—that is, if the old lady and gentleman really are Lord and Lady Mannington, as Vi seems to have discovered ; " and he proceeded to tell the story circumstantially, though without this time making fun of Lady Mannington, as he had done before.

While he talked his mother's face brightened every moment ; tears of gladness came into her eyes, and at last she clasped her hands together in an ecstasy of joy.

" O Geoffrey, my brave boy ! " she cried. " Supposing the train had come a moment sooner—only supposing ! Thank God, it did not ! But what did my—what did they say to you about it ? "

" They hadn't time to say anything, because the train was just off. They did send a footman to fetch me, but at that moment the guard began shutting the doors, and we both jumped into our respective carriages, only I had to get out again for the wretched cur. Lord Mannington tried to say something when I chucked it in, but he couldn't, because the train was moving. Besides, there was a young lady in the way."

" But how did Violet find out who he was ? "

" I haven't a notion."

" I wonder—can he have been here ? " thought Lady Harriet.

Just then Frederick came in with some coals.

" Has any one called lately—any stranger—while I was out, to see me or Mr. Geoffrey ? " she asked.

" No, my lady. There was an old gentleman come one day, and asked for Mr. Geoffrey Montgomery; but I said there was no one here of that name, only our Mr. Geoffrey, which his name was Treean."

" What did he say then ? "

" He said he s'posed he'd made a mistake, and he must write, and then he went away."

This was Frederick's first place as a full-blown footman. He had previously been a page in the country, and a long speech was a great effort to him. So, having now delivered himself at such length, he hastened to beat a retreat before more questions should be asked.

" Treean ! " repeated Lady Harriet; " he can't have understood. And so he has been to the house, and I never saw him ! "

As she spoke thus to herself she suddenly remembered Geoffrey's presence.

"Geoffrey dear, I want to tell you something," she said.

"Yes, mother. But I think I know what you are going to say. Lord Mannington is your father."

"Yes. But how did you know?" she asked, startled, and yet relieved that she was spared the explanation.

"Oh, I heard it at Eton, from some fellows who made out that they were my cousins. I felt rather an ass at first not to know my own grandfather's name, but I supposed you didn't want me to."

"It was not that exactly; it was only that it was such a painful subject. I ought to have told you, though, before you went to school. I didn't think of your meeting relations there. But though he is my father, I have not seen him or—or—my mother for seventeen years; and now they are in London—only a stone's-throw from here."

She gave one of those little sobs to which any sudden access of distress gave rise, and then was silent a minute, while Geoffrey sat by, not knowing what to say.

At last Lady Harriet looked up.

"It is right I should tell you, Geoffrey, why I am parted from my parents in this way. It is—because —because—"

" You married father, and they didn't like his having no money except what he made by his work. I suppose that was it, wasn't it?" suggested Geoffrey, anxious to make it all as little trying for his mother as he could.

" Yes," she replied: " it was not Claude—it was not your father himself that they objected to; that would have been impossible. But I was their only child, and they had formed such hopes and plans, and then I thwarted them; and my father is very strict in his ideas of obedience between child and parent. Perhaps he was right. But my dear, dear mother—it nearly broke her heart, and sometimes I think it will break mine."

She could say no more. The old wound, thus opened afresh and to her own boy, was more galling, more distressing than ever.

Geoffrey watched her suffering with a wild tumult of conflicting emotions warring in his own heart.

" The old curmudgeon," he said to himself, " to bear malice all these years, and just because father—the grandest, most splendid fellow—hadn't a lot of miserable tin! To deprive his wife of her only child, and his daughter of her parents for seventeen years! Faugh! It's enough to make one sick of money and grandeur. I *wish* I could help mother; but how can I? Poor thing—and with all father's illness upon her too! And there are those two old Crœsuses rolling

about in carriages, with flunkies by the dozen, and
more money, I daresay, than they know what to do
with.   All the same, it's not my business to blame
them."

He rose from his chair, and went up to Lady
Harriet.

"Mother," he said, as he bent down to kiss her,
"I'm awfully sorry; but after all things are no worse
than they were.   I daresay Violet didn't let out who
she was yesterday."

"Yes, she did; but she didn't see my father.   She
says it was a tall man she spoke to, and he is small
and slight."

Geoffrey burst into a shout of laughter—he could
not help it—and at the sound of his merriment even
Lady Harriet smiled through her tears.

"Isn't that like old Vi?" he said.   "She works
away like a mole in a hole till she thinks she's
sniffed out the whole secret, as she calls it, and then
she goes and tells her story—which is a pure invention—to the wrong man.   That is the best joke I
ever heard in my life.   Can't you fancy Vi, mother,
with her nose in the air, and her most important
manner, marching up to a tall old stranger, and
announcing that a perfectly unknown animal, named
Geoffrey, was sorry he had thrown a dog at Lord
Mannington's head!   He must have thought her a
raving maniac escaped from the nearest private asy-

lum. It is the richest thing I ever knew. How I *will* chaff Vi! I made it pretty hot for her this morning, when I found she had been telling lies."

By this time Lady Harriet had quite recovered her equanimity. She considered a moment, when Geoffrey finished speaking, whether his intention ought to be carried out, or whether she should forbid Violet's conduct to be made the subject of a joke.

"But I can't tell Claude about it yet," she thought; "and until he settles what is to be said to Violet, I do not like to take any decided step. Perhaps it is just as well that she should be laughed at for her ridicu- lous self-importance and curiosity. But she shall not be persecuted."

She turned to Geoffrey, who was on the point of departure.

"You can 'chaff' Violet, dear, but I will not have you unkind to her. I do not wish to go into the matter thoroughly until your father is able to advise me; but as far as I understand it, Violet denies having told a falsehood. And until you are perfectly sure of another person's wrong-doing, you have no right to treat her as guilty. Besides, it is not your place to judge or punish your sister."

Geoffrey's face clouded. He remembered with com- punction what he had said that morning to Violet. His mother noticed his change of countenance.

"What have you said to Violet?" she asked.

"I said she was a li—, that she didn't speak the truth; and I told Gerry to send her to Coventry," he answered, twisting the door-handle uneasily.

"Geoffrey! how could you?"

"Well, mother, I didn't know. It all seemed very shaky. But I'll tell Gerry to leave off again. I don't want to be hard upon Vi."

"No; 'judge not, and ye shall not be judged.' Remember that, Geoffrey dear."

"Yes, mother. I'll go and put it all right; but I don't feel sure about old Vi all the same."

"No, nor I," said Lady Harriet to herself as he left the room. "There is a hardness and a reticence about her which show me that she is concealing something still. It is a sore trial, but I must be patient, and, please God, one day things will come right."

On leaving his mother, Geoffrey proceeded to the school-room; but Geraldine was all alone there.

"Where's Vi?" he demanded.

"Gone upstairs. She is very angry with you. And, O Geof, must I really send her to Coventry? It is so dreadfully difficult. I keep forgetting every minute."

"No; mother says we're not to do it. She's not sure that Vi has been fibbing, so of course it would be a shame to punish her till it's quite certain. In England a criminal is always assumed to be innocent until his offence is absolutely proved," said Geof with rather a grand air.

" Yes, of course," responded Gerry with entire conviction. If Geof had asserted that Charles I. had been beheaded in 442 B.C., she would unhesitatingly have answered, " Yes, of course."

Geoffrey now went up to speak to Violet. He knocked at her door, and a very cross voice said,—

" Come in."

" It's me, Vi," he said, advancing into the room; " and I've come to say that I'm sorry I called you names just now, and we're not going to send you to Coventry—at least not yet."

Violet did not seem to be particularly gratified by this conciliatory address; in fact she looked extremely angry.

" I don't care what you say," she answered. " If you really believe what you said in the school-room, I shouldn't think you'd ever want to speak to me again. Anyhow, I don't want to talk to *you*, so you can go away."

This was not encouraging, but Geoffrey reflected,—

" Of course she's rather savage at what I said—any one would be. I must try and make it up with her presently."

Meditating thus, he departed, much to Violet's relief.

XV

MR. TREHERNE'S INDIGNATION.

GEOFFREY'S precious preparation-time ran quickly away, and the last few days arrived all too soon.

He certainly had worked hard for the three weeks since Christmas. Without foolish cramming at unreasonable hours, he had worked methodically, according to a system he and his father had planned between them, so that he should have plenty of the recreation and exercise which were indispensable to his keeping well.

During the last fortnight Mr. Treherne had been feeling better, and seeing his boy's earnestness and energy in the difficult task he had chosen for himself, he had announced his intention of helping him. Lady Harriet expostulated in vain. She reminded him of all Sir Lewis's dreadful predictions if he went on working his head; she added her own fears, but it was of no use.

"Nonsense," he said: "reading these old classics will be play to me, and I shall like to refresh my acquaintance with them. I haven't opened some of them since my own university days, when I had them at my fingers' ends." (Mr. Treherne had been a First-class man, and a Fellow of his college.) "Studying a brief, or getting up a speech on a difficult case, *is* work, but not running through Tacitus or Thucydides with Geoffrey. Instead of hurting me, I believe it will do me good, and prevent me from thinking so much about myself."

So Lady Harriet had to give in; and when she saw the delight it gave her husband to go over the old ground with so intelligent a pupil as Geof, she rejoiced that she had done so.

Mr. Treherne had that talent—strange to say, rare in clever people, common in less gifted persons—of imparting knowledge intelligibly and helpfully. He was a born teacher, and Geoffrey felt at once the immense advantage it was to him to go through the books with so excellent a scholar and so efficient an instructor. He gave up the "coach," and worked entirely under his father.

But, alas! a fortnight is a very short time, and the daily lessons came to an end almost as soon as they began—at least so it seemed to the enthusiastic and eager lad.

As soon as her husband's first alarming symptoms abated, and he became partially convalescent, Lady Harriet felt that a painful and most disagreeable

task must be gone through: she must tell him of
Violet's conduct.

Mr. Treherne was very strict in his ideas of pro-
priety, and exceedingly averse to girls putting themselves forward in the slightest degree. He was fond
of quoting the French proverb: *La femme est une
fleur qui ne donne son parfum qu'à l'ombre.* Knowing this made Lady Harriet's work all the more
difficult. However, as it had to be done, there was
no use in putting it off. So on the evening of Geoffrey's first lesson, when, after having some tea in the
library, he was expatiating on the pleasure it was to
impart knowledge to so teachable a boy, his wife
said—

"I wish Violet were as satisfactory as Geoffrey!"

"What do you mean?" inquired Mr. Treherne.
"You can't expect her to have such abilities; Geof
is unusually quick. But what has she done that
is unsatisfactory?"

The ice thus broken, Lady Harriet plunged into
her story, and as she saw the frowns which gathered
on the listener's forehead, and heard his expressions
of annoyance and indignation, she half wished she
had kept silence. When she reached the part about
Violet's visit to Hyde Park Gardens, Mr. Treherne's
anger broke out altogether.

"Do you mean to tell me," he said, "that after your
parents have refused to hold any intercourse with us

for seventeen years, because I committed the enor-
mity of marrying their daughter, the first time they
come to London a child of mine has forced herself
into the house all alone, and insisted on button-holing
Harry Armadale, in order to pour out a cock-and-bull
story about something which is Chinese to him, and
has given her name as Violet Treherne at the end?
Upon my word it is unbearable! *I*, who have
rigorously abstained from obtruding my unwelcome
personality on a father-in-law who hates me for what,
if it is a fault, is one of which he was once as guilty
himself—my love for you; *I* to be now thrust on his
notice in the person of an impertinent, meddling little
minx like Violet! No doubt he thinks—for of course
he has heard the story from Armadale—that I sent
her. What does she mean by it? Really, Harriet,
I hope you have punished her severely. What have
you done?"

"Nothing yet, Claude. I didn't like to until I
knew what you wished."

"If I were well, I would send for her this moment,
and tell her what I think; and I am half inclined to
as it is."

"Oh no, Claude dear, pray don't! It will worry
and excite you so dreadfully. Besides, she has gone
to bed by this time. I will say anything you tell me
to-morrow."

"Then you can tell her that I am extremely displeased with her, and that I desire that she will stay in her room and have her meals there for a month from to-day."

"A month! O Claude, that is such an immense time! Say a fortnight; surely that will be enough."

"Well, we go away to-morrow—that is Wednesday —to stay till the end of the month. She shall come down again the day we come back, but not any sooner."

Lady Harriet felt that she could expect no further relenting, so she had to submit, feeling very unhappy at the thought of the humiliation which the punishment would entail on Violet.

"And just when we are away too!" she thought. "It will be quite as much a punishment to poor little Gerry. How dull she will be, with me away, and no Geoffrey or Violet to speak to downstairs!"

After a great deal of persuasion from his wife and the doctor, Mr. Treherne had been induced to go down to Brighton for a few days' change of air. Geoffrey was to go too, that he might not lose his father's help, and to proceed thence to Oxford the day before his examination.

"Poor Gerry!" he exclaimed on the morning of his departure, as he said good-bye, "I'm awfully sorry for you. One can fancy a ravenous man without food, or a miser without his money, but imagination fails when asked to picture Gerry without a victim to pour out her eloquence upon.—Mother, I hope you have remembered to order tongue for dinner each day while Gerry is alone.—Oh, and I say, Gerry, you can write to me every evening, you know. That will be splendid!"

"Can I really, Geof? There won't be very much to say, you know. But I should like to so much, if you wouldn't laugh."

"Laugh! Why, it will be of the greatest use; I shall be most grateful. I shall want no end of old waste paper to pack my things in—boots, you know, and so on, for Oxford."

With this Parthian dart he ran down the steps, and Gerry, half-angry, half-pleased, had only time to call out—

"You'll telegraph to me, *won't* you, about the scholarship?" when the carriage drove off.

In spite of all Geoffrey's efforts to make things up with Violet, that young lady was so deeply offended and hurt by all that had occurred—still persistently maintaining to herself that she had acted quite properly, and had been shamefully ill-treated—that she had determined finally to send the rest of her family to Coventry; which she accordingly did, to Geoffrey's great amusement, and to her own exceeding discomfort. Sulky people inflict infinitely more disagreeables on themselves than on other people.

But her resolve certainly was a very unpleasant

one for poor Gerry, now she was entirely left to her own devices.

"Fancy being glad the holidays are over, and that Miss Newman is coming back! That is something I never did expect to feel," she reflected drearily, as she mounted the stairs with slow, listless steps, after the departure of the rest of the family. She was not fond of lessons; no intellectual pursuit had any great charm for Miss Geraldine Treherne.

XVI.

AN UNEXPECTED ENCOUNTER.

THE day before the scholarship "exam" was a momentous one for Geoffrey. When he first awoke he could hardly believe that the time he had been working for so hard that the last month had seemed like a year was now actually at hand.

It was five A.M., and still night, when he first opened his eyes. Leaping out of bed, he performed his toilet with marvellous rapidity, and then with furious ardour fell to reading certain marked portions, chiefly of choruses in his Greek plays, which his father had deemed likely to be set.

By the time that breakfast was announced—the bell had not been rung since Mr. Treherne's illness—Geof's brain was nearly "fuddled," as he himself expressed it, by the intensity of his application; and if instead of the matutinal meal the examiners had been waiting for him then, his chance of success would have been small indeed.

Some eight hours later, with the good-byes and good wishes of his father and mother still ringing in his ears, he found himself whirling off in an express *en route* for the "ancient and noble university" of Oxford.

He leaned back, and tried to realize his situation, it all seemed so wonderful. A few weeks ago he was a school-boy, with what appeared a long vista of school life still before him. Now he was a man, or at least just going to be one (this was what Geoffrey thought), and taking his place in the arena of active endeavour.

That transition from school to university is so great a change to a youth! At such an age nothing seems impossible. The unimaginable future, dim and shadowy, broods over a world still wonderful as in the days of chivalry or fable, and gilds with fictitious splendour the sombre tints of life.

In the train Geoffrey had sense enough to abstain from fatiguing his mind with futile efforts to work. On the contrary, he tried—not unsuccessfully, as it seemed to the fellow-travellers who heard his subdued chuckles—to interest himself in *Punch*. But as he gradually approached Oxford, his excitement increased, until he found it more and more impossible to think of anything but his impending arrival.

He had never before visited the famous university town; but he had heard much of the glories of its colleges and historical buildings, and vague visions of architectural marvels floated through his head. The reality, it must be confessed, struck him at first with a feeling of disillusion.

The station seemed just like all other stations, nor could any majestic sense of the presence of the refining evidences of a remote antiquity be discerned in the features of the porter who transferred his luggage to a cab, and gazed disdainfully at sixpence.

The streets, too, through which he was conveyed struck him as "seedy," to say the least; and half-a-crown did seem rather a high price to have to pay for the pleasure of traversing considerably less than a mile of them. Still, he felt something of the thrill he had anticipated when his hansom drew up at the porch, and he saw through the gates the outermost quadrangle, gray, silent, and deserted, with the old walls looking down upon it like the shell of the cenotaph of the past.

It was some days before the commencement of the Lent term—an unusual time in which to compete for a scholarship; but the one Geoffrey had entered for had been vacated unexpectedly, and the college authorities had their reasons for filling it at once. St. Nicholas, where Geoffrey had, through his father's interest, obtained rooms, was therefore a howling wilderness, tenanted only by a few college servants, the ancient and estimable Provost, his executive officer the Dean, and one Fellow.

Upon the latter, as, according to the porter, the

only dignitary to be found, Geoffrey proceeded to call, in the hope of obtaining some information as to the examination to be held the ensuing day. He had yet to discover the profound indifference with which one Fellow of a college regards the administrative duties which fall within the province of another.

Mr. Parleau was a short, stout, middle-aged man, with a military carriage, deeply learned, and entirely bald. To Geoffrey's first hesitating knock at his door—he lived on the second floor of " No. Four Staircase," and his " oak" was not sported—no answer was returned; and it was not until after repeated and somewhat louder raps that a voice within bade him enter.

The room in which Geoffrey now found himself was large and lofty; but as the only light in it was derived from a small shaded reading-lamp fixed to an arm-chair, it was nearly half a minute before he discovered the figure of Mr. Parleau, who was standing like a statue in front of the extinct fire, with his hands behind his back, and his chin resting on his shirt-front. He was in evening dress, but wore a large black bow-tie.

There was something so uncanny in his perfect motionlessness, and the dead silence he maintained, that Geoffrey, albeit not prone to shyness (what Eton boy ever is ?), felt confused and at a loss how to begin. He stood near the door, with his hat in his hands.

"I came," he said—"I ventured to—I thought perhaps you would—"

"Be good enough to shut that door."

Geoffrey turned his head with a start, and perceived that he had failed to fasten the inner latch. He complied with the request, or rather command, and then waited, in the hope that Mr. Parleau, having regained the gift of speech, would now continue to use it, and so relieve him from his embarrassment. He waited in vain, however : Mr. Parleau maintained his sphinx-like demeanour, and the silence became more oppressive and appalling than before. Geoffrey began to wish that the floor would kindly open and permit him to pass through it. But as this was not likely to happen, he felt that he had better make one more effort.

"I came," he began once more, and then paused again, fairly "floored," as he said to himself, by the "rumness of the whole thing."

"You made that statement before," said Mr. Parleau; "it is apparent, and superfluous. Proceed."

"I—I beg your pardon," continued Geoffrey, stammering painfully from sheer nervousness; "I—I understood from the porter that as the term had not yet begun, you might possibly be disengaged at this time."

"You have yet to learn that a student—a man of letters—is never disengaged, in the sense of being

ready to play the fool with the first idler he sees.
And when I am what you call 'disengaged,' I am re-
cruiting my brain with rest and quiet. Are you
aware that the noise you have been making at my
door was simply inhuman ?"

Geoffrey could think of no reply to this speech but
" What utter rot !" And this he felt was not a suitable one, so he held his peace.

" I am still ignorant of your object in coming here,"
observed Mr. Parleau, after a few moments, in a voice
which clearly said, " and I wish you had stayed
away."

" I am in for the scholarship to-morrow," said
Geoffrey, trying to pull himself together, " and I
thought you would perhaps be kind enough to tell
me something about it."

" May I ask who directed you to apply to me for
information ?"

" No one, sir," replied Geoffrey, flushing. " I only
came to you because the porter said every one else
was out. I am very sorry if I have done wrong."

Mr. Parleau deliberately removed the shade from
the lamp, put an eye-glass into one eye, and fixed his
visitor with a cold and fishy stare.

" You appear very young," he remarked calmly.

At that moment Geoffrey certainly felt so ; but he
only answered, " I am not very old," staring wildly at
Mr. Parleau's bald head as he spoke, with an instinc-

tive feeling that there was a retort somewhere, if he could but get at it.

" What is your age ?"

" Sixteen, sir. I shall be seventeen next May."

" By whose advice do you offer yourself for this scholarship ?"

" My father knows the provost, and he wrote to him, and put my name down," answered Geoffrey hesitatingly.

" And may I ask what your name is ?"

" Treherne, sir. You may have heard of my father perhaps. He is well known at the bar."

Geoffrey always mentioned his father with a funny little assumption of dignity. He had a very poor opinion of himself, but he felt that a sort of reflected honour belonged to him as the son of one who in his judgment had no superiors and but few equals. However, as the introduction of Mr. Treherne's name had not always the electrifying effect which Geof considered it ought to have, he was rather astonished at the way in which Mr. Parleau received it.

" Treherne !" he repeated, coming several steps forward, and speaking in a very excited voice—" did you say Treherne ?"

" Yes, sir ; Geoffrey Treherne."

" Are you at Eton ?"

" I was, sir, till the end of last half ; but now I have just left."

What could Mr. Parleau be thinking of? His voice grew louder, and his manner more agitated. With each question he drew a step nearer to the spot whereon his visitor, still nervously turning his hat round, was standing.

"Do you—do you know—I think you do—a boy named Harry Eastover?" was the next inquiry made by the learned Fellow, now actually speaking with almost a stammer.

"Eastover? Yes, rather, sir. I saw him only the other day—just before we went down to Brighton. He'd almost got well of his sprain, and I expect by this time he's gone back to Eton. All the fellows were to go last week."

"If that is the case—I mean if you are the Eton Treherne who knows Harry Eastover—I am under the deepest obligations to you," said Mr. Parleau, in a tone of the heartiest friendliness and cordiality. As he spoke, he came still another step nearer, and shook Geoffrey warmly by the hand. "Come and sit down by the fire. No; I'm sorry I can't say that. It's gone out—all my fault, absent-minded book-worm! But come and sit down, and I'll tell you who I am."

Feeling as if this must be some extraordinary dream, and he should be waked up suddenly in a minute by banging his head against the wall, or some such startling catastrophe, Geoffrey obeyed.

"I am a married Fellow," continued Mr. Parleau,

"or rather I was; but now, I grieve to say, I am a widower. I used to live in the town, and only occupy these rooms during the day. I have had several children; but I have lost them all, one after another—all, that is, but one. Each one has been of a consumptive tendency, and not one has lived beyond ten years old. My only child at present is just eight and a half. By special favour he is allowed to live here."

"Then I trust he'll keep well, and get over the dangerous age. Is he all right at present, sir?" asked Geoffrey, forgetting his wonder at being made the recipient of these family disclosures, in his sympathy with the bereaved husband and father, whose melancholy voice and manner now contrasted forcibly with his previous snappish demeanour.

"Yes; so far he has only shown a general delicacy, not any symptoms of a specific malady. But I never part with him—at least I had not until last month, when I let him go to visit an aunt in London. After what occurred there, however, I shall never allow him to go from here again without me."

"Why, sir? what happened?"

"Simply that, from all I can hear, he very nearly bled to death. He is a peculiarly intelligent boy, accustomed to the companionship of scientific and intellectual people; and I gather that at my sister-in-law's house he was neglected, grossly neglected. On the day the accident took place every one was out—

even the butler—gone to some trifling party of pleasure, and the poor child was left without a soul to speak to, to amuse himself. He is of an inquiring disposition —all clever children are—and he wished to discover whether it was true that the contact of steel with human flesh really produced injury to the cuticle, and hemorrhage, as he had often been told when desired not to play with sharp instruments. To carry out his experiment, he went into the dining-room, and taking up a carving-knife from the luncheon-table, he put his left hand down on the flat surface, and dealt it as smart a blow as he could. The blade was very sharp, the handle a heavy silver one, which made the knife come down with the more force, and the result was a severance of three of the fingers at the second joint."

"Why, that's just like little Frank, Eastover's cousin," cried Geoffrey; " but he has got all right, sir, so I hope your little boy will."

" My little boy's name is Frank, and he *is* Eastover's cousin," said Mr. Parleau; "that is precisely my point."

Geoffrey got very red, and again wished he could take refuge in a sudden disappearance through the floor.

"Treherne," went on Mr. Parleau, rather rapidly, " I heard what you did that day, and what an effort it was to you to do it. The doctor tells me that there are a considerable number of persons constitutionally averse to the sight of blood, and that from your birth you have been one of them. Therefore, I am the more grateful to you for your unselfish, manly behaviour. If, as might easily have happened in the middle of the day in London, no doctor had been available for some hours, my boy would have owed the future use of his hand, and perhaps his life, to you. He is far too weak to lose blood with impunity—as it is, he is cruelly pulled down; but if the bleeding had not been stopped as it was by your timely measures, I cannot bring myself to dwell on what might have happened."

Poor Geoffrey! how he hated all this "palaver"! He had not the faintest idea what sort of answer he ought to make.

"I'm awfully glad," he said at last, "that he got better so soon. But I really did nothing; the doctor came almost directly. Frank was a plucky little chap, and behaved like a brick. Where is he now? I heard he had gone home, last time I saw Eastover."

Mr Parleau took up a bedroom candlestick.

"I'll show you, if you'll be very quiet," he said; and he led the way to an inner room, trying to be very noiseless by walking on tiptoe, but failing entirely on account of his very creaky boots.

There, up in the corner, on a small iron bedstead, lay the sleeping figure of the little boy who was the object of so much love and solicitude to his lonely father.

"Poor little chap! he still looks very white," said Geoffrey, touched at the anxious, wistful look which overspread Mr. Parleau's face as he felt the child's pulse and drew the bed-clothes round him.

"Yes, but he never has much colour. I think and trust he is mending," he replied, speaking very low, and carefully shading the light of the candle with his hand.

In a minute they went back to the sitting-room, and Mr. Parleau continued—

"I was rather irritable just now, I am afraid, Treherne; but every one here knows that Frank goes to bed at seven o'clock, and is a very light sleeper, so that nobody ever knocks at my door unless they wish to annoy me. They open it, if my 'oak' is not sported, and ask to come in; and if it is, they know I don't want to see any one."

"I see. I'm sorry I didn't know," said Geoffrey, rather relieved at this explanation of his host's peculiar reception of him.

"And now about this scholarship," proceeded Frank's father: "how can I help you?"

"I thought perhaps, sir, you could tell me what time the 'exam' is to begin, and where it is to be held. And then, if it is a fair question, I should like to know what order the papers are likely to come in."

"As to the two first points, you must consult the dean, in whose charge are the arrangements; they do not fall within my province. You might just catch him now before dinner," he added, consulting his watch.

"Then I had better go at once," said Geoffrey, rising.

"And with regard to the probable order of the papers, it is quite uncertain, but I think I may say that as a rule the 'comps'" (the pieces of English to be converted into Greek or Latin prose or verse) "are set towards the close of the examination."

"Thank you, sir. Then I will say good-night, and I hope Frank will very soon be as well as ever."

"Oh, but you must be my guest while you are here. Will you come to luncheon to-morrow? I'm afraid my breakfast-hour won't do for you before the 'exam.' By-the-by, I was just going to Hall; but what do you say to dining here with me instead?"

"Thank you, sir—you're very good; but I think I had better keep quiet to-night, and just have a last look at one or two things," replied Geoffrey gratefully, though he was too "fresh" to appreciate adequately the distinction which such an invitation conferred upon him.

"Well, perhaps you're right. I won't press you. But remember, whenever you have time for a meal here, I shall be delighted to see you to breakfast or luncheon, and so will Frank. You made quite a conquest of him. He is always talking about what 'Treherne said.'"

" Is he ? " said Geof, laughing ; " he's the first person who ever did me such an honour. But I should like very much to come to luncheon, if there is time after the morning 'exam.' It would be no use to try and work up between whiles. If I went in tired I should only come a greater howler than I expect I shall now."

" Oh no, I hope not. *Nil desperandum,*" said Mr. Parleau ; and Geoffrey departed to seek out the other college magnate.

XVII.

A CHAMBER OF TORTURE.

THE Dean of St. Nicholas, whom Geoffrey next
proceeded to interview, proved to be an altogether different type of man from Mr. Parleau. He
was a short, sharp, decisive personage, with energetic
and peremptory manners. Though perfectly courteous,
he managed to convey to his visitor in about two
minutes that he was of rather less importance than an
individual shrimp. This unpleasant truth is indeed
the first piece of knowledge usually imparted to a
freshman by dons. The reverse of it can only be
arrived at by those who, in obtaining some intellectual
or athletic distinction, eventually confer a lustre on
their college. Such fortunate beings bask in the
smiles of their superiors; but, alas! they form a very
small minority of the "members of this university"—
or any other.

Mr. Standforth, Dean of St. Nicholas, looked search-
ingly at Geoffrey when he heard the errand on which
he had come to Oxford. He was one of those embar-
rassing people who always give one the impression that

they are " summing one up"—reading one's character, and detecting as by intuition all its weak
points.

Like Mr. Parleau, the dean inquired Geoffrey's age
and the name of his school.

" It's perfectly absurd for you to think of sitting
for such a thing," he said.   " You have no more
chance of winning it than that lamp.   I don't want
to discourage you; go in and try it by all means—it
will show you your own shortcomings, at all events; but
to come up straight from Eton—*Eton*, of all places!"
Geoffrey looked up indignantly, but reflected instantly
that poor Mr. Standforth had evidently not had the
privilege of being an Etonian, and so spoke in ignorance.   " What could make you think yourself a likely
person to obtain it ? "

" I don't know, sir, but there are one or two other
Eton fellows going in, and I think I have read as
much as they have."

Geoffrey's frank, cordial manner, even to this ex-
ceptionally unsympathetic person, would have thawed
nineteen professors out of twenty.

" What have you read ? "

Geof mentioned the classical authors on whom he
had bestowed his attention of late, adding with a
modest confidence,—

" And Plautus; I hope I shall get that to-morrow.
I really do think I am pretty well up in him."

"*In*deed! do you really?" responded Mr. Stand-forth with profound sarcasm.

"I mean," said Geoffrey, colouring again, "I've read the plays a good deal, and I've been using some awfully good notes."

"*In*deed," said Mr. Standforth again. "May I ask whose?" He put the question with a sudden eager-ness which contrasted strangely with his previous abruptness and frigidity.

"It's awfully dense of me," said Geoffrey, looking puzzled, "but I've forgotten the name. Oh, here is the book in my pocket. I had some idea of reading it in the train."

As he spoke he pulled out a small volume and handed it to his inquisitor. The latter's brow cleared in a marvellous manner as he looked at it.

He "hemmed" twice loudly, as if to mark the change in his disposition.

"And you have found these notes useful?" he said in an inquiring manner.

"I should think so, sir. I never saw anything like them. I only wish I'd such good ones for all the other books."

Mr. Standforth hemmed again, as if involuntarily expressing some inward emotion, and a close observer might have noticed that a faint flush, as of supreme satisfaction, overspread his face.

"Sit down," he said; "take that lounge chair by

(164)   11

the fire" (he deposited himself in his own arm-chair as he spoke), "and tell me how I can help you," he went on. "What is the special information you require?"

Geoffrey told him the points upon which he sought enlightenment, greatly wondering at the dean's alteration of demeanour.

"I haven't bound up *his* little kid's fingers," he said to himself; "it's something to do with Plautus, but what, I can't imagine."

However, he listened gratefully as Mr. Standforth explained that the examination was to begin at half-past nine o'clock in the college hall, and to continue for some four days. When he finished speaking Geof rose to go.

"Thank you, sir," he said, taking up his hat, but not venturing to offer his hand.

Mr. Standforth rose also, and smiled benignly.

"I sincerely hope," he observed, as he insisted on shaking hands with a warmth which amazed his visitor, "that you will get Plautus to-morrow, and succeed in winning the scholarship. Oh, here is your book."

"Oh, I mustn't forget that," said Geoffrey, as he pocketed the volume. "I mean to have one more look at some of the stiffest bits to-night."

"I really do hope you will succeed," said Mr. Standforth, with a fresh access of benevolence, following his visitor to the door, and pressing his hand affectionately a second time.

"Thank you, sir, very much. I hope I may," rejoined Geoffrey, and he departed, marvelling secretly whence arose this sudden solicitude for the unlikely success of a hapless Etonian with "no more chance than a lamp."

"What *could* make the old boy change like that?" he thought. "It was all in a moment, after I gave him my Plautus. Could it have been something in that, I wonder?"

He took out the book, and examined it curiously, as if it had been a talisman. Seeing nothing remarkable on the cover, he turned to the title-page, and there read the words, "With Introduction and copious explanatory Notes by A. J. Standforth, M.A., Dean, and late Fellow, of St. Nicholas College, Oxford."

"Oh, *that's* it, is it?" he exclaimed. "No wonder he was mollified. How he must have swaggered inwardly while I was holding forth on the splendours of the work! I'm afraid, though, in spite of his Plautus notes and all father's coaching, I haven't a ghost of a chance. Still, I may as well have a shot as I'm here. Nothing venture, nothing have. Besides, I'm no worse off if I do fail."

After a solitary meal of a substantial nature—for nothing ever seemed able to impair Geof's appetite—he went for a little stroll, and not even the thought of the morrow could take away the strange charm which belonged to this first night spent within the college walls.

Perhaps England possesses no spot more weirdly lovely than the cloisters of St. Nicholas, when the moonlight falls on the green gardens they enclose— a perfect lawn of smoothest grass, still and silent as if haunting fairies slept upon the turf, and yet embedded, not amidst the forest trees where Oberon of old sported with Puck, but amidst historic walls coeval with bygone ages and forgotten men. All around, figures cunningly carved by long-vanished hands look down upon the sward, on which they have gazed now for centuries; and in the unbroken quiet of vacation-time, when no riotous sound of mirth falls jarringly upon the night, the place and scene resemble a court of some enchanted palace, where all life has been turned into stone, and the sleeping beauty waits to be awakened by her destined knight.

So at least it seemed to Geoffrey as he paced to and fro in the deep stillness, passing alternately from patches of dark shadow to areas of silvery light, as the moonbeams cast their fitful light upon the grass and the statues.

All sorts of thoughts and fancies came to him in that solitary vigil. To his excited imagination the past seemed to live again. He thought of the great men who in former time had walked where he was walking now, and who had made their names and that university famous to all posterity by their deeds or their writings, and he inly vowed to strive with his whole soul to add, if he could, one more name to that roll of renown.

At 9.30 A.M. the next day, Geoffrey found himself waiting on the steps leading up to the college hall, in company with some two-and-twenty other youths bent on the same mission as himself. The portals were at length flung open, and he entered a chamber big enough for two hundred men to dine in it, and more than lofty in proportion.

There was of course no crowding, nor any of the trouble usually experienced on a first day in the schools, in finding the little separate tables appropriated by name to each individual.

A competition for a college scholarship is indeed not a university examination at all, and it generally differs also from the latter in being conducted on much more favourable lines as regards creature comforts. Here every man took what place pleased him at the mighty boards which in term-time nightly groaned under the weight of the food necessary to satiate the hunger of young Oxford, while all possibility of mutual help was averted by the distance which separated each aspirant from his fellow.

In an examination for a scholarship all the papers are " unseens "—that is, no books are given beforehand for the candidate to read up, and he must consequently take his chance as to whether he possesses any previous acquaintance with the portion of Latin or Greek given him for translation. Of course, though, the wider the reading, the greater the chance. Geoffrey was in luck. All three of the extracts in the first paper, which proved to be Greek unseen, were known to him. The first was from the "Phædo" of Plato, which he had gone through with his father, with whom it was an old favourite. The next was from Thucydides, and was followed by what looked like a childishly easy piece out of Xenophon's "Anabasis," but which on closer inspection proved to bristle with pitfalls for the unwary, which former experience alone enabled him to avoid.

If he had trusted to Mr. Parleau's prediction as to the order of the papers, and had reserved any private " tips," as is sometimes done with fatal result, to be looked up in the intervening hours, he would have been " done " indeed, for " Latin Prose " was the heading of the paper which awaited him in the afternoon. The piece of English given for translation was that gorgeous passage in Lord Beaconsfield's "Tancred" beginning, " Why are there no more kings ? " etc. It was all about Solomon and the Queen of Sheba, flat-nosed Franks, and northern morasses, and in his private capacity as a novel-reader Geoffrey had often hugely admired it. His admiration, however, was changed to loathing on the present occasion, when he had to wrestle fiercely with the immense difficulty of turning such sonorous sentences into equally majestic Latin, and when all sorts of latent ambiguities of meaning revealed themselves to his distracted gaze. At last, though, the task was achieved, and Geoffrey could fairly feel that the result was not unsatisfactory.

We need not follow him through the rest of his paper-work, which lasted three days. It is enough to say that when he had finished them he felt, to use his own phrase, that he had "floored them" pretty well. The question was, Would any one else have done better? His agony was not quite over. He still had the *viva voce* to go through. But that proved less of an ordeal than he had expected, for Mr. Arkwright—once an Eton master, and a special friend of Geoffrey's—turned out to be one of the examiners. Geoffrey could not tell whether he recognized him or not, but as soon as he beheld his familiar face, he felt more at home and less nervous than he had been before.

When the *viva* was over, and Geof had emerged from the chamber of torture, it was nearly one o'clock, and very cold and dreary. Now the excitement was at an end, he felt what he called "washed out," and indeed he looked it. For all these consecutive days he had been on the tip-toe of anxiety, conscious of how much depended upon the result of this examination. And now there was nothing to do but to wait for the publication of his fate, his usual hopefulness died away, and he could remember only the mistakes he had made.

XVIII

SUSPENSE.

GEOFFREY had availed himself of Mr. Parleau's invitation, to come whenever he liked, several times since the day of his first visit, and had always been most hospitably received and welcomed. It was therefore with a sense of relief that he turned now towards the Fellow's rooms, sure of sympathy and, what was of hardly less importance, of a solid meal.

Mr. Parleau was very kind, and listened with exemplary patience while Geoffrey minutely detailed all the intricacies of the examination that morning, and recounted the errors into which he had fallen, or thought that he had.

"My chief bit of luck was at the beginning of the *viva*," he said. "The examiner was an old Eton master—he only left the year before last—so I wasn't half as nervous as I expected."

"Do you mean he spoke to you and let you know that he recognized you? That was very unusual and irregular."

"Oh no, sir; he didn't give me the slightest sign

of recognition. I don't mean that. But he was a particularly stunning old boy at Eton; he and I always got on, so I felt all right as soon as I saw his face."

"Who were the others? I suppose there were three?"

"Oh yes; the three Furies or Fates, or anything else you like to call them. One had a long white beard, and looked about a hundred and ninety; and the other was a perky little fellow, who caught you up every time you showed the slightest symptom of tripping, like a woman's knitting - needle with a dropped stitch."

"I can knit," suddenly announced Frank, who was not used to being thus left out of the conversation. He had now finished his luncheon, and wished to make his friend Treherne give him his attention.

"Can you?" said Geof; "then I wish you'd knit me some cuffs. I had a pair on yesterday morning, and I took them off when I was writing, because they got in the way; and like an ass I left them in the hall. Of course no one knew anything about them to-day."

"There is something, then, for you to do for Treherne, Frank," said his father. "You ought to be very proud of such a commission."

"I'm not proud," said Frank crushingly, "'cause it's very wrong to be proud.—But I'll make the cuffs,

Treherne, 'cause it'll be good-natured; and I'm very good-natured, and such an original. I heard Mrs. Sherwin say so yesterday."

"What colour are the cuffs to be? Something original, please, Frank," observed Geoffrey, hoping that Frank's wools were in some far-distant spot to which he would retire, and leave him to talk to his father in peace.

"Oh, I know. They shall be gamboge and pink; that will be lovely.—May I go out now, father, and buy the wool?"

"Not by yourself," said his father. "You can go and ask Mrs. Sherwin if she is going out shopping this afternoon, and will take you.—Mrs. Sherwin is the porter's wife, and a great friend of Frank's," explained Mr. Parleau, as his son departed.

"What time do you think the result of the 'exam' will be announced, sir?" asked Geoffrey, who was simply on tenter-hooks until he knew his fate.

"I don't know," said his host; "but I should think by four o'clock."

"It's half-past two now. I think I'll go for a walk, and then I shall be at hand as soon as there is any-thing to see."

"Or, in plain English, you mean to hang about the schools from now until dusk, or until the list is out, eh?" said Mr. Parleau, seeing through this transparent little scheme with the eye of an expert.

"Well, sir, I do so awfully want to know," responded Geoffrey, looking rather shamefaced.

"Oh, I don't blame you ; I was just the same at your age. Go along, and I hope you'll have good news written on your face when you come back."

So off started Geoffrey. He did not have a very cheerful afternoon for the next two hours, especially as, go where he might, the words, "You have no more chance than that lamp," rang in his ears. It was a depressingly raw, damp day, and the wind was what Geoffrey called a "north-beaster." He turned up his coat-collar till it reached his ears, and began what he really did mean should be a smart walk. But before he had gone half-a-mile some unseen lode-star drew him back, and made him retrace his steps, until he found himself standing before the door on which the scholarship paper would be nailed.

As he drew near he saw two more shivering human beings coming up, and in another minute four others appeared. If he had not recognized them as his fellow-competitors, he would soon have perceived that their errand was the same as his own. For though they walked along with a sort of studied negligence, and did not appear to take any interest whatever in the oak door which was the evident object of Geoffrey's frequent glances, a close spectator might have seen that, whichever way they walked backwards and forwards, they never failed to gaze earnestly towards the door as they passed it. Having had a good look, Geof turned round and made another manful attempt at a walk which should make him acquainted with the beauties of Oxford. But the same fate befell him again. It was only a quarter to four when he once more found himself, very cold and rather wet, for a slight drizzle was now falling, outside the mystic door.

By this time a small crowd had gathered there, composed of the twenty-two youths who had gone through the examination with our hero. Their remarks would have amused the latter at any other time, but now he was too much absorbed in his own thoughts and desires to care much for what went on around him.

"I think I'm pretty safe," observed one young man with a very sharp, sallow face, and little, eager black eyes. "I've never failed for anything yet, and I don't see why I should begin now."

"Considering that twenty-two fellows out of twenty-three must fail, I don't quite see why you shouldn't be one," remarked a candid friend.

"*I* go by the school a fellow's been at," said a third speaker; "there's more in that than in the individual himself. It's form that tells in your work more even than brains. Form's the great thing."

"Yes," responded another: "if you talk of *schools*, I think four of us shall run each other pretty close. Wykhamists always did distinguish themselves more than other people."

"Wykhamists!" cried a listener, in a tone of scarcely veiled contempt; "an old place like that is all very well for traditions, and so on; but for real work and real form give me a comparatively new school—like Uppingham, for instance; that's *the* place."

"You are an Uppingham fellow, I imagine," replied the ruffled Wykhamist."

"Yes, sir, I am, I am proud to say."

"So I should have thought," responded the Wykhamist, in the voice of one who would say, "*There* is a retort for you!"

But the Uppingham champion did not look the least withered. On the contrary he gave a sanguine glance at the door, and moved a little nearer to it.

Geoffrey now joined the small knot of talkers.

"It's much the best plan to take these things coolly," said a fat young man with a snub nose, who wore an ulster which reached down to his feet, and was adorned with sealskin collar and cuffs. "My motto is Don't worry yourself about anything; it isn't worth it. Now I don't care a hang whether I get the scholarship or not; it won't make the slightest difference to me, and therefore I'm all the more likely to win it."

There was a hum of disapprobation at this speech, but every one was too polite to say what he thought. Nobody looked anxious, however, that the easy-going, sealskin-coated young gentleman should turn out right in his views.

" I don't care about the money," he continued ; " it's only the *kudos* of the thing, and after all that isn't much.—*You* look as if it was a matter of life and death to you," he added, turning to Geoffrey with a patronizing air which was not agreeable.

" Yes ; I can't say that I am as completely indifferent as you," he replied. " I confess, though I know I haven't the faintest chance, I should like to win."

" What's your school ?"

" I was at Eton," said Geof shortly.

" Ah, I thought as much. So was I. An Eton man has an unmistakable look, I always think. But I see you don't remember me."

" Yes, I do. I think your name is Griffin," answered Geoffrey, looking at him steadily.

Griffin turned very red as he met his eye.

" Yes," he said hurriedly. " I didn't stay very long. Place didn't agree with me—too great a mixture too —went abroad instead, to see the world and study modern languages."

Geoffrey recollected Griffin's sudden removal on account of his having been mixed up in a bad row in the town, and thought it kindest and wisest to say no more.

At that moment a man appeared in front of the door with a paper in his hand, which he proceeded to

nail up.   How every one did push and jostle that unfortunate person !

"One moment, *if* you please, gentlemen," he said;
" it won't make things better for no one to push me
off my legs."

"Stand back!" cried Mr. Griffin authoritatively—
"stand back, and let the fellow do his business !"

By way of showing a good example, he squeezed
as close up to the man as he could, that he might
get the first look when the important paper became
visible.

Geoffrey was at the back, so that he could only tell
who had *not* got the scholarship by watching the
disgusted faces of the unsuccessful candidates, who
walked away one after another, until he got near
enough to look.   By this time the hubbub of voices
had a little subsided, and he distinguished a sound
which sent a thrill all through him.   It was a familiar
name.

"Who is he ?" asked some one.   "He wasn't at
Uppingham; that's all I know."

"Who has won ? who has won ?   Oh, do tell me!"
cried Geof, quite frantic at last.

"Treherne—a man named Treherne.   Who is he,
I wonder ?   Hullo, my dear fellow ! don't faint; it
isn't worth it.   We're all in the same boat; only one
could win."

For the revulsion of feeling and the shock of joy,

following his hard work and his week of suspense, had been too much for Geoffrey, and he had turned suddenly giddy, and fallen against the man next him, not one of those who had been talking.

"It isn't that," he said; "but *I'm* Treherne, and I am so awfully glad."

"I'm sure I'm very glad you've got it then, as it couldn't be myself. I see I'm *proxime*, so we've run each other pretty close. But I congratulate you heartily, and I wish you success in your university career."

"Thanks very much," said Geoffrey, taking the other's proffered hand; and then he felt that he must go at once and bear this glorious news to Mr. Parleau. So off he darted, but on his way he remembered his promises about telegrams. He was passing an office at the moment, and he went in and despatched a message to Brighton.

"There," he said to himself as he came out, "if ever any one had reason to be thankful, I have. I shall wait to telegraph to Gerry till to-morrow, and concoct something special."

It was not the honour of the thing only, though no one of Geoffrey's age was likely to be blind to that, which made him rejoice so intensely, but the consciousness of having done something which would give his father such supreme pleasure as he knew this little bit of success would bring.

"He's coached me himself," he reflected delightedly.

"I do believe this will go a long way towards curing him."

"I congratulate you," cried Mr. Parleau as Geoffrey appeared in his room a few minutes later.

"Yes; isn't it *rippin'* !" said Geof. "But how did you know?"

"Know, my dear fellow! Why, it's written on your face as plainly as that is painted," pointing to a Gladstone bag with three great white letters on it; "and it does you infinite credit, in my opinion. Most of your rivals must have been older than you, and probably they had all had a longer preparation. I think you have reason to be proud of yourself."

"Oh no; it's father's coaching, I know that," said Geoffrey, "and it's partly my luck in the *viva*. They gave me just the bits I knew."

"If you hadn't known any bits, they couldn't have done that," observed Mr. Parleau, determined to take the best view of things. After this, seeing how tired Geoffrey was, he let him alone; and he spent an hour in a big arm-chair by the fire—Frank being out—weaving fancies, and building castles in the air, which, now he was in so happy a mood, were all of the most magnificent description.

That evening, when he had the honour of dining in Hall, he found himself quite a lion in a small way. Term had begun again that day, and there were a good many men up.

The great point which seemed to strike every one was his extreme youth, as exhibited in his personal appearance. It had never been a subject of special delight with Geoffrey, but he comforted himself with the reflection that the magnates at the high table were comparing him with themselves.

" And the youngest of them must be thirty at least," he thought, with deep pity for people so far advanced in life, " and some of them even more."

Mr. Standforth was ecstatically delighted at the result of the examination. He almost embraced Geoffrey when the latter told him that he had had Plautus, and had been able to manage the passage given entirely through knowing the dean's note upon it.

After an hour or two spent with Mr. Parleau, Geoffrey went off to bed, for he felt as if sleep would do more to set him up again than anything else.

XIX

"*I SAW YOU WERE ONE THAT SPOKE THE TRUTH.*"

IT was Geoffrey's duty as newly-elected scholar to call the next day upon the provost of St. Nicholas. He went in the afternoon (not daring, in his ignorance of Oxford ways, to go earlier), and was received by that potentate very graciously, and invited to luncheon. He did not like to decline the invitation, in case that should be an infringement of some time-honoured custom, but he said to himself,—

"What a horrid bore! That will just prevent me from getting home to-night, or even before the evening to-morrow. I meant to be there as soon as father and mother, and now I shan't. However, the old boy means well, so I must grin and bear it."

He spent the morning with Mr. Parleau, and told him why he had allowed himself to be kept another day.

"He was nearly sure to ask you," he observed; "but you were not obliged to go. You might have said you would have gone down before that. However, it's just as well you should lunch there now when there won't be many others, and then you'll get to know something of the provost. He's worth know-ing, you'll find; every one is fond of him."

"Then I think I'll say good-bye, sir, and just go to my rooms and put up my things," said Geoffrey. "Then I can start by the three o'clock train. Thanks most awfully for all your kindness and hospitality to me. You have made my 'exam' week a great deal jollier than I expected it to be."

"I'm very glad I was here," said the other. "And mind you come and see me when you come into resi-dence. Frank will have got his cuffs finished by that time."

"Oh, long before. Look!" said Frank, holding out two knitting-pins, quite different in size, on which about two inches of his gamboge and pink wool were visible. "I'm a wonderful hand with my needle. I heard Mrs. Sherwin say so yesterday."

"It strikes me that you hear Mrs. Sherwin say a great many silly and undesirable things," observed his father. "I shall try and get another companion for you—some one of your own age."

"Ask father to send Leonard; he would just do," said Geoffrey. "He'll be nine next month, and he's going to leave the school he's at now at Easter."

"Is he? Well, I'm not sure that I shan't write to him then.—Frank, you're fast becoming a spoiled child."

"I'm not. I'm a dear pet, and full of droll sayings. Mrs. Sherwin says so," responded Master Frank in an offended voice.

"I say, Frank, is your trumpeter dead?" asked Geoffrey as he shook hands. "I think he must be, for you do nothing but sing your own praises. Good-bye; and don't chop any more fingers off before I see you again."

So saying, he went away, and before long he was seated in the provost's dining-room, feeling younger than ever as he listened respectfully to the words of wisdom which fell from the learned and venerable don's lips.

The meal, though intended to be bountiful enough, was not wholly satisfactory from a material point of view to Geoffrey. He was distinctly hungry; but no one seemed to contemplate the possibility of a second help of either meat or pudding, and so he had to content himself with the wing of a chicken and an infinitesimal portion of Genoese pastry, his eyes fixed meanwhile on a round of cold roast-beef and a Stilton cheese which graced the sideboard, but apparently only as ornaments, since neither the provost, his wife, nor his daughters, showed any sign of offering them to Geoffrey or the one or two other guests present.

He came away directly after luncheon, but he was only just in time to catch his train. Indeed, he had to get a porter to fetch his ticket, for he found that his watch was slow by station time.

He had made up his mind to travel third class for the future, though, like most Etonians (luxurious beings as a rule), he felt that such a proceeding was rather *infra dig.*

"Still," he reflected, "it hurts nobody but me; and now father isn't well off, why should I spend his money on a thing that does nobody else any good, and only lasts as long as one's in the train?"

His carriage to-day was very full; but as the train was a parliamentary one, and stopped at every single station, much to Geof's disgust, the people kept continually getting in and out, so that by the time the junction was reached where every one had to change, Geoffrey was the only passenger who had started from Oxford.

Just as the train arrived at the station before the junction, a man next the window said, "We'd better get out our tickets; they're all looked at here."

His male fellow-travellers began rummaging about in their pockets, and those of the gentler sex in the holes of their gloves,—of course to find that the ticket had tumbled out, or had got so far in that the glove had to be dragged off in a great hurry and fluster.

Exactly at the moment that the ticket-collector appeared at the door, all the tickets, having been passed up by their various owners, were in the possession of the man who sat by the window, and he handed them to the collector.

The latter counted them, and then looked up sharply.

"There's one short. Some one hasn't given me a ticket," he said.

Every one answered, "It wasn't me; I know I gave mine."

Geoffrey felt in his pocket.

"I know I had a ticket," he observed, "because I was late, and the porter brought it to me when I was in the carriage. I feel almost sure I passed it up."

"I'm positively certain *I* did," cried every one else in chorus.

"No one can say *I* hadn't a ticket, considering I give you about a dozen," remarked the man by the door rather loudly, looking round the carriage with a defiant air. "Whoever's bin cheatin', 'tain't me, any'ow."

Geoffrey was the only one who had not stated positively that he had given up his ticket, and yet he felt that he must have done so, only he couldn't remember it. He searched diligently in every pocket, but all in vain. The collector began to grow impatient.

"I'm not going to wait here all day, nor keep the train here till you've found it, so I just tell you," he said, "you must make up the money among you from where the train started from, and that's Birmingham."

There was a loud outcry at this.

"Why, I only got in two stations back," said one. And another rejoined,—

" I've only come from the last one of all."

The man at the door, who had come from the next station but one after Oxford, observed,—

" The young gent over there's come the furthest, and he's the only one as don't remember a-giving up of his ticket."

" I believe I saw you give it, sir," said an elderly man at the further end of the carriage, speaking for the first time since the discussion began; " and for my part I am quite ready to pay my share of the missing ticket."

" No, thank you," said Geoffrey; " I will pay it—at least, if I have enough," he added, flushing. " I suppose I ought, as I can't actually recollect for certain about it, especially as I have come the furthest. What will it be ? "

" Nine and five."

" Oh, then, I can do it," and he produced a sovereign, which was speedily changed, and a paper given him which he was to show at Paddington. Before the collector closed the door he gave a searching look at the man who had delivered up the sheaf of tickets, and said,—

" You've done the trick this time, mister; but take care you don't try that dodge once too often."

The man pretended not to know that the words were meant for him, and he took no further part in the conversation which went on among the other passengers for the remaining few minutes before the train stopped at the junction and every one got out.

It was now nearly five o'clock, and all the lamps were lighted. Geoffrey was very cold, and stayed by the waiting-room fire until the London train arrived.

When he got in he observed that the same elderly man was in his carriage who had tried to help him before. He was the only one of the old fellow-passengers there, and as he and Geof were at different ends of the compartment, they did not enter into conversation.

Geoffrey had invested in an evening paper, and for the first half-hour he was too much engrossed in it to notice who came in or went out.

He became conscious, however, after some time that his two opposite fellow-travellers took a very evident and obtrusive interest in his personal appearance. They were two young men, rather flashily dressed, with their hats a little on one side of their heads, and they were studying a paper very eagerly, and whispering to one another, apparently about something they saw in it which was very exciting.

What possible connection there could be between Geoffrey and a newspaper paragraph he could not imagine, but the behaviour of his *vis-à-vis* became so disagreeable at length that he took the trouble to look and see what their paper was.

"Why, it's the same as mine—the *Evening Stan-*

dard," he said to himself. "Perhaps I can find the wonderful bit that seems to have so much to do with me. It's in the agony column, I think." He turned his own paper to get at the front page, and as he did so he heard the young men say,—

"It's him; I'd lay anything it is. Look—'dark hair, straight nose, brown eyes, quick, alert manner, dark-gray ulster.'"

Just then Geoffrey found the place, and running his eye down the second column he came to these words:

"Left his home—A lad about seventeen, tall, good-looking, dark hair, straight nose, brown eyes, quick, alert manner, dressed in a dark-gray ulster. Slight hesitation in speech, and a scar on left temple. Whoever shall bring information which shall lead to the recovery of the same by his friends shall receive a reward of £100. Apply —— Office, Strand."

Geoffrey turned perfectly crimson with embarrassment and indignation. He felt that the description was most unpleasantly applicable to himself. Perhaps these men were detectives in plain clothes. "Good gracious, what a horrid combination of circumstances!" he thought.

He looked up, and found the eyes of both the two men fixed upon him. He saw that they knew he had read the advertisement.

"Well," said one of them familiarly, "so you're caught, you see. It's no use trying to go on with the little game. Bolting don't answer in these days. The resources of civilization's one too many for you, as the Grand Old Man says."

Geoffrey tried to speak, but the more he tried, the more impossible it seemed to find the right words. What *could* he say? If he denied being the person of whom these men were in search, how should he make them believe him? However, in the face of being supposed to have a "slight hesitation," instant speech was imperatively necessary.

"So here goes," thought Geoffrey. He looked steadily at his opposite neighbours, and said distinctly,—

"I am not the person you evidently think me."

"Oh, *in*deed!" answered one man. "I'm sorry to hear you say that, because we shall be obliged all the same to watch your movements until we deliver you up into safe keeping at the —— Office. A hundred pounds isn't to be sneezed at in these hard times."

"All I can say is that I utterly deny having run away from home. I have just been to Oxford to sit for a scholarship at St. Nicholas, and I am at this moment on my way home."

"Yes; it's a nice little story enough, but we're not quite so green as you'd think," said the young man rudely.

Every one in the carriage had become silent, and was listening to this extraordinary colloquy.

"I can tell you my name, if you wish it, and who my father is. As for the scar on the temple, you can see for yourself."

But there he stopped short, for he suddenly recollected that the day when he fell down after binding up Frank's hand his head struck against some sharp corner, and for several days he had had a mark on his forehead. He had not noticed it lately, but it was possible it might be there still. He had taken off his hat, and put on an old cricket cap, that he might lean back more comfortably. He felt that if he had a scar it must be visible now; hence his sudden hesitation.

"Yes, your temple—I should just like to have a look," said the second man, putting out his hand as though to take Geoffrey by the shoulder.

The latter drew himself up haughtily.

"Be good enough not to touch me," he said; "if you do, I'll give you in charge for assault, at the next station."

"No: keep quiet, Jack. Don't let us put ourselves in the wrong," murmured his companion hastily.

Just then the train stopped at another station, but no one got in.

"Let me ask you one thing, sir," said a voice from the corner, and every one turned that way. It was the elderly man who spoke.

"Certainly," replied Geoffrey courteously.

"Will you give your name?"

"By all means. My name is Treherne, and my father is one of the best known barristers in England."

He pulled out two envelopes.

"Here you may see that my letters are directed to G. B. M. Treherne, and also that they are addressed to me at St. Nicholas, where, as I told you, I had been for a scholarship 'exam' until yesterday."

"Your name may be Treherne, for all we know. But how are we to tell that isn't the name of the very young gent we're after?" asked one of the men. "*That* won't do, gov'nor."

"Did you win the scholarship, sir?" asked the elderly man, undoing his own newspaper, which he had folded up some time before.

"Yes, I did. But I don't see what that has to do with the suspicions these fellows have got in their heads."

"Only this, that I saw a paragraph headed 'Oxford' just now. I didn't read it, but no doubt the scholarship you speak of is mentioned; and if your name is there as the winning candidate, that proves your story to be true, as I believe it to be. What was the name of the scholarship, sir?"

Geoffrey told him.

In another minute his champion silently handed the paper, which was a *Morning Post*, to the young men, pointing triumphantly to the paragraph which an-

nounced that Geoffrey B. M. Treherne had been elected
Scholar of St. Nicholas.

The men's expression on seeing this was not one of
pleasure. They only made one more effort—a very
feeble one.

"It's in your own paper, and you saw it, and said
that was you."

"If you think so, pray look through my paper and
see," said Geoffrey; "but be quick, please, as we are
nearly at the terminus."

He handed them his *Evening Standard*; but after
the most diligent search they could find nothing about
Oxford scholarships.

While they were looking, Geoffrey crossed over and
sat by the elderly man who had twice befriended him
so opportunely. There were only three other people
in the carriage now besides the obnoxious young men.

"I am very much obliged to you," said Geof, "for
your support."

"Oh no, sir—not at all," he said. "I knew you
were speaking the truth, because of the way you
behaved about the ticket just now. I saw then you
were one that 'spoke the truth whichever way it
might tell—whether for or against you."

Geoffrey only said again,—

"Well, I'm very much obliged to you," and added,
"It might have been a disagreeable enough business.
Do you think they are detectives?"

"Detectives? Bless you, no, sir. They wouldn't be so insolent if they were doing their duty. No; you may depend they're a couple of young good-for-nothings trying to pick up a few pounds without working too hard for them."

Just then the train stopped, and the young men, having concluded their fruitless examination of the paper, made no effort to detain Geoffrey, as, after bidding good-bye to his friend, he left the carriage.

In another two minutes he and his portmanteau were deposited in a hansom, and he was speeding homewards through the lighted streets.

XX

LADY MANNINGTON'S DINNER-PARTY.

POOR Lady Mannington! her life was a very dreary one. Anybody who knew what a cruel blank the parting from her only child had caused would have thought her attachment to a "wretched cur" less ridiculous than it appeared at first sight. Hers was a nature prone to love and to care for others—full of sympathy and demonstrative affection. She was always more fond of the sickly children and the ill-used wives in her own village than of the strong happy ones.

Some six years after Harriet went away, and her very name had by her father's order ceased to be mentioned, Lady Mannington's coachman drove by accident over a puppy, which had run just under the wheels of the advancing carriage. The animal was taken up, apparently dead or dying, and Lady Mannington, shocked and penitent for what was really no one's fault but the victim's, insisted on its being put into the brougham, in which she drove home at once, that the sufferer's wounds might be attended to.

Everything was done which could be thought of, even
to securing the daily attendance of the nearest farrier.
After some time of suspense, Gyp rewarded the care
bestowed upon him by recovering from all his injuries,
except the fracture of a front paw. This he always
held up pathetically, slightly curved, in a way calculated to enlist the sympathy of every one who
saw him.

His sufferings and his supposed patience so won
upon Lady Mannington that she declared she could
not part with him; and her husband, who did occa-
sionally feel some compunction for the shadow his
pride and ill-temper had cast over his once cheerful,
light-hearted wife, gave way, and let her keep the
dog as her companion and friend. Perhaps he felt
bound to do something to lessen the loneliness his
own conduct had brought about; perhaps he wished
to get back the lost serenity of his home. At all
events, he bore the manifestations of affection lavished
on Gyp, and the exasperating amount of pet-dog talk
addressed to him, with extraordinary patience.

Lady Mannington, whose whole being had been
wrapped up in her only daughter, seemed now to
pour out the wealth of her pent-up love upon the
lame mongrel. But foolish and fussy as she seemed,
she had not really found consolation or forgetfulness
of her child in her fondness for the dog. Her life
was still a dreary round of emptiness, dominated by

one feeling—dread of her husband's wrath. She loved and admired him more than any one else, knowing him to be far cleverer and larger-minded than herself. But she feared him also, and she shrank with terror from reawakening the storm which had burst over her head and Harriet's, when the engagement was announced which disappointed the ambitious projects Lord Mannington had formed for his daughter.

On the evening of the day on which Geoffrey had been enduring his last examination-torture at Oxford, there was a dinner-party at Lord Mannington's house in Hyde Park Gardens. It was of a mixed description, for Lord Mannington, who had views of his own on all subjects, considered that asking people in "sets" was a mistake.

"If you want to be bored to death," he said, "invite your guests because So-and-so and So-and-so think alike, or will 'get on' together. That is quite fatal to any amusing conversation. They will both take the same general view of a question, and then split hairs about petty details, and on these miserable trifles they will squabble all dinner-time; whereas no one else cares a rap about such minute shades, or even knows that they exist. A mathematician and a dancing-master would get on together fifty times better than a couple of scientists with 'views,' or a brace of philanthropists with schemes for the regeneration of mankind. No; you should always ask the most dissimilar people to meet each other."

"Very well, dear. Tell me who is to come, and I will write the cards," replied his wife meekly. She always obeyed "Ralph," and by this time most of his hobbies were well known, though this particular whim was new.

Lord Mannington had not come to London, except for a few days, for many years—in fact, not since his daughter's marriage, when he had sold his house in town. His own country neighbourhood was like many others: dinner-parties perforce consisted of what was to be had in the way of people; there was little scope for selection of the fittest. This year he had suddenly taken it into his head to come up and hire a house for the winter; and now he had arrived, he displayed a wonderful amount of friskiness, and a desire to renew old friendships and make new ones which quite surprised his wife.

The party gathered round the table on the parti-cular evening with which we are now concerned included a high and dry Tory cabinet-minister; a very advanced Radical M.P. and his wife; Mr. Arkwright, Fellow of St. Austin's College, Oxford; and a lady named Miss Singleton, who spoke a good deal on women's rights, was a member of the School Board, and of the Board of Guardians, and had been a wrangler at Cambridge. She wore large round spectacles, which she turned full upon any persons who ventured to argue with her, eying them with a stare of pitying scorn if they dared to enunciate reasons for differing from her opinions.

She had been holding forth now upon the paramount importance of a scientific education for children.

" There is nothing," she said, " to be compared with it. The old plan of filling the memory with facts and figures, and not cultivating the reasoning faculties, is quite exploded now."

" Is it really ? Ah, I did not know that," said Mr. Arkwright, with the air of one seeking enlightenment on a wholly new subject, which surprised and delighted Miss Singleton.

" Oh yes," she continued : " it is universally admitted now that young children's education should begin with Euclid and logic. That teaches them to think and reason almost before they have learned to spell, and then the bare facts of history, etc., can easily be acquired later, and as they are imparted to the children they will think them out. The one great essential is that they should be able to reason for themselves, and, as Buckle says, live in a state of inquiring scepticism—accepting nothing that is not proved."

" It is a profound system, and to me, at least, it has the additional merit of novelty," observed Mr. Arkwright.

"But may I ask where the culture of the moral faculties comes in? Or is the necessity for that also exploded?" inquired the minister, with a slightly satirical intonation, which, however, was quite lost upon Miss Singleton.

"The moral faculty?" she repeated disparagingly. "Oh, that is a different thing altogether. It has to do with other perceptions, other powers than those of the brain and intellect."

"Still, I suppose you would teach a child something of the value of truth, and unselfishness, and generosity——I mean you would at least mention the existence of such virtues?"

"Well, you know, I am a great enemy of didactic teaching. I should let a child deduce or infer that the practice of such qualities was admirable or expedient, from the events of history and a careful course of reasoning upon the occurrences of life."

"I see," responded the minister, glancing at the Radical M.P. to see whether even he went as far as this very "progressive" lady. But he would not commit himself to any opinion on the subject.

"I wonder," said Mr. Arkwright, "whether a lad I saw to-day, who interested me a good deal, had received his moral instruction in that way. I should be inclined to say not. Yet he certainly had imbibed it very thoroughly and efficiently."

"Who was he, Arkwright?" inquired Lord Man-

nington. He had what he called "set off" Miss
Singleton by a skilfully worded challenge, but since
then he had only been listening silently with cynical
amusement as she explained her views.

"Who was he?" repeated Mr. Arkwright. "Oh,
only a young fellow from Eton, who came up to sit
for a scholarship. It was the first thing of the kind
he had tried for—he is but sixteen. I was rather
struck with him to-day, partly because I had known
him before, and partly because he looked so supremely
young that it seemed quite absurd that he should be
standing for a thing which would turn him at once
into an Oxford 'man.' I didn't much think he would
get the scholarship, but I knew it would be a near
shave, for his paper-work was very good—he wrote
such a capital essay on 'What makes a Hero'—but
there was another fellow who had done almost as well,
and very often the questions are a mere matter of
luck. A man may have a bit he has specially worked
at in his papers, and be entirely floored in the *viva*."

"And was this boy floored?" asked the minister.

"No, my lord; quite the contrary. He did capitally, and I began to think he was safe, though his
rival had done well in that particular book too—it
was Tacitus. I said something about his knowing it;
and he looked up and said, 'Yes, I know that bit, but
I'm not at all up in the end part.' I didn't say anything, but just put him on in a later part. He

construed the passage without a mistake; and then
he said, 'I suppose I ought to tell you that those two
bits and one other are just the very parts that my
father went through with me last Monday.' 'Well,
here's one more,' I said, and I turned over a page or
two. He positively laughed—I never saw any one
laugh during a *viva* before—and he remarked, 'And
that's the third. What awful luck!' Then he went
ahead, and you know it would have been absurd to
try again. It wasn't my affair that I had chosen his
three show bits, and I only knew it because he had
more truth and openness about him than any other
fellow I ever saw before."

"What a dear darling boy!" cried Lady Mannington, who, like several of the other people, had listened
with great interest to this anecdote. "I hope he has
got the scholarship, Mr. Arkwright?"

"Yes; I am glad to say he has. I was half afraid
he would not, for there were two other examiners
besides myself, and they leaned a little towards the
other man. But when we were talking it over,
Parleau, one of the Fellows of St. Nicholas, said he
knew all about my *protégé*, and that the scholarship
really was of some importance to him, for without it
he would probably not be able to go to Oxford. As
it did not matter so much to the other, it was finally
given to the Eton fellow. His work certainly did
him great credit, for he must have been quite three

years younger than his rival, and no one else came near those two."

"Do you say he was at Eton?" asked Lord Mannington. He had listened with a good deal of attention since Mr. Arkwright had begun his story, and now the cynical expression Miss Singleton's remarks had called forth was gone.

"Yes; and you have seen him, Lady Mannington, I know," he said, turning to his hostess.

"*I* have seen him? I don't remember having seen an Eton boy—at least to speak to—for years."

"Don't you recollect being at the Windsor Station last December, when your dog ran on to the line, and one of the boys who crowded the station jumped down just as the train was coming, and saved it? I was there, and I thought it was such a plucky thing to do."

"Remember it, Mr. Arkwright! I should think I do. And I've never been able to thank him from that day to this. We have tried every way we could; —haven't we, Ralph?"

"Yes; I have made many efforts. So he and this honourable young fellow you tell us of are one and the same! That makes me all the more anxious to make his acquaintance. What is his name, Arkwright?"

"Geoffrey Treherne. He is a son of the famous barrister whose health has broken down from over-pressure. I saw, though, in the paper to-day that he is rather better. I always liked the boy; there is something so hearty and straightforward about him."

He talked placidly on, not noticing the electrical effect which his words had upon his host and hostess. Lady Mannington turned pale, and her husband bright crimson. She asked the gentleman next her for a glass of water, and Lord Mannington poured himself out a glass of wine.

Fortunately the guests were not old friends, and no one recollected the name of their host's married daughter, so that though several people saw the emotion caused by Mr. Arkwright's words, only conjectural conclusions were formed as to their special significance.

As soon as Lady Mannington had drunk the water, she made the signal for rising, and in the drawing-room she soon recovered her equanimity. Gyp was there, of course, and the enthusiasm with which she stroked his bristly back and shook hands with his lame paw amused the ladies of ordinary minds as much as it disgusted the more advanced intelligence of Miss Singleton.

The remainder of the evening seemed very long, but it came to an end at last. The moment the latest guest had said good-bye, Lady Mannington walked up to her husband, and laid her hand upon his arm.

"Ralph dear," she said in a tone of intense though suppressed feeling, "what do you say now?"

"I say that such a boy is worthy to be owned as my grandson; and I shall go and see his father, in order to tell him that it is his son's honour and courage and modesty that have made me forgive him for dashing all my dearest hopes to the ground."

"But he is ill, Ralph. Did you hear what Mr. Arkwright said?"

"Yes; I asked him all about it afterwards. I have quite made up my mind what I shall do, and to-morrow I mean to do it."

XXI

GERRY'S VISITORS.

THE days of her parents' absence passed drearily enough to Geraldine. She had never before been really glad to have lessons to do, as she was this week.

The unsmiling face of prim Miss Newman was a welcome sight in the school-room now. With all her love of her own voice, Geraldine really could not address remarks to the chairs and tables, so that Miss Newman (though she never listened by any chance, and only threw in an occasional "Yes" or "No," or "Indeed," when the stream seemed to flag) was a great deal better than nobody, as a companion to the lonely Gerry out of school hours.

A great deal of her time was passed in writing to her mother and Geoffrey; but she was painfully conscious of a lack of interesting events to chronicle in these epistles. Any little piece of news she could pick up she utilized. And one day she was able to announce: "I saw Geoffrey's old lady to-day. She was in the park, and the same footman was on the carriage, and the same dog (that must be Geoffrey's terrier—I mean the one he saved) was sitting with his head at the window; and I could see the lame paw hanging down, all curly and useless. He looks a cross dog and much too fat. I wish Geof had been there; but he wasn't," etc., etc.

That is a fair specimen of Gerry's letters; they always contained a large percentage of "ands." They gave her unmitigated pleasure to compose; it is to be hoped they gave her correspondents equal amusement to read.

Violet meanwhile sat, silent and injured, in her own room. Miss Newman had suggested that lessons would relieve the tedium of the day, and Violet had grumpily consented to write a few exercises and do some sums. She went out walking every day with the maid—a promenade she hated more than words could tell, for she felt as if every one must be wondering why such a big girl was walking with a servant instead of a governess; and when she saw any one coming whom she knew, she dreaded so unspeakably lest they should ask her where Miss Newman was, that she would go miles round to prevent a meeting.

"It is all part of the cruel persecution to which I am subjected," she said to herself. "How I wish I had left Geoffrey's affairs alone! I'll never try to help any one again." She would not add, "nor meddle in other people's concerns."

And so the time went slowly by; and at last came the day of Geoffrey's examination. Poor Gerry! She was in such a state of excitement that Miss Newman did not know what to do with her. At one moment she was quite certain that Geof would win, and come in far ahead of every one else; and the next she was in a state of despair, saying that she knew he would fail, and then his heart would break with grief.

"And father's too," she added lugubriously. "I know the stronger he grows the more his old anxiety that Geof should get on will increase. And mother says the sea air has done wonders for him. I'm so glad! But oh, I wish I knew what Geof is doing at this moment!"

That day passed, and the next—the day of the *viva voce*. On the following day Gerry came downstairs very nervous, but in a state of moral "strut," for she expected a telegram all to herself; and common as that missive is now, it had never yet happened to Geraldine to receive one.

She got through her morning lessons somehow, and then, as it was a very wet day, she sat by the school-room fire with a story-book, while Miss Newman retired to Violet's apartment.

"Not that there would be any good in going to see Vi, if she wasn't at lessons," thought Gerry; "she's so cross. I wonder how long she'll be like this. I *couldn't* do it, not if I were offered a thousand pounds. Hark! What's that?"

It was a loud ring at the bell, and she listened breathlessly while some one went to the door.

There were voices, but whose Geraldine could not tell, as the school-room door was shut. They seemed to come nearer—to pass the door—to go to the drawing-room. And then she heard some one shut the door, and a minute after Frederick came in and said,—

"The Earl and Countess of Mannington, miss, in the drawing-room."

"*What?*" said Geraldine, hardly believing she had heard aright.

"The Earl and Countess of Mannington," repeated Frederick stolidly.

"But—but—you must say that every one's out—away—not here," answered Gerry, so flustered that she could scarcely speak.

"I did, miss; but when I said Mr. Treherne and Lady Harriet was away, they asked for Mr. Geoffrey; and when I told 'em he was gone too, they asked to see Miss Treherne. Which I didn't like to mention Miss Violet bein'—bein'—"

He stopped, at a loss how to express his meaning with proper respect, and Geraldine cut in instantly.

"Oh, but, Frederick, what *can* I do? Do you mean that they are sitting on two chairs at this moment, expecting me to go in and see them?"

"They was standing up when I left 'em, miss, but

by now they may be sittin' down, which I should think one of the sofas 'ud be a likely place. But they're lookin' for you to go and speak to 'em. I'm certain of that. They wouldn't take no denial."

"Oh, how *dreadful!*" cried Gerry, thinking, in a perfect frenzy, of her inky fingers, untidy hair, and very tumbled sateen apron, with one pocket hanging by a single stitch.

Frederick looked sorry for her, but having done his part, he went away without more words, and Gerry tore upstairs to try and make herself presentable.

"O Vi," she cried, as she dashed into the room, regardless of Miss Newman's presence, "who *do* you think has come?"

Violet only grunted in an uninterested sort of way.

"Why, Lord and Lady Mannington!"

"*No!*" exclaimed Violet. "O Geraldine, how extraordinary!" She was quite shaken out of her sulks by this unlooked-for intelligence.

"Yes. I can't *think* what they can want," observed Gerry, as she dried her red hands, smoothed her hair, and tore off her apron. Then she flew downstairs, leaving Violet in a state of curiosity and anxiety quite indescribable.

Opening the drawing-room door, Gerry saw a fat old lady and a little thin old gentleman seated near the fire opposite each other. They both rose as she entered, and looked at her eagerly. She saw that they expected her to shake hands, which she accordingly did. Just as she had thus greeted the old lady, she caught sight of a black-and-tan terrier, and without thinking a moment she cried out,—

"Why, that's Geoffrey's terrier! He said it had a game leg, and so it has. Poor little dog! what has happened to it? Why, you must be Geoffrey's old lady. Oh, I am so glad."

Geraldine was a slightly-built child, with a pleasant, open face, and a peculiarly nice voice. She looked so natural and so pleased as she spoke that Lady Mannington was quite delighted, in spite of being called an "old lady."

"Yes, dear," she answered. "This is my little Gyp, who owes his life to your brave brother. We have tried for a long time to find out his name, but we only succeeded, by accident, last night."

"I wrote to him five weeks ago," said Lord Mannington; "but I suppose my letter did not reach him. What is his second or third name?"

"Montgomery. He is Geoffrey Bentham Montgomery Treherne, and he is the eldest of us all, and the nicest, and best, and cleverest. Oh, I can't tell you what Geoffrey is. He is quite unlike any one else."

Gerry's voice and manner showed that she was now mounted on a well-trained hobby, and could go on as long as breath was given her, or there were listeners to hear what she said.

"How many are there of you altogether?" inquired Lord Mannington in a gravely interested voice.

What a grand, what a unique opportunity for the loquacious Gerry! I need hardly say that in about ten minutes, during which Miss Geraldine Treherne had the conversation entirely in her own hands, Lord Mannington was made aware of the exact age and name of each of his grandchildren, with the date of their birthdays, and the addresses and special characteristics of their respective schools. He was also told what the relative forwardness or backwardness of each was in Gerry's estimation, and the opinion entertained of their recent progress as evidenced by Miss Newman's dictums and the boys' school reports.

Gerry had no idea of her own relationship to her visitors, as Lady Harriet had requested Geoffrey not to explain until her return home. She did not know what reports Gerry's thoughtless speeches might not give rise to amongst the servants.

Gerry had begun to feel a slight sensation of fatigue in her voice, when Frederick suddenly entered the room, bringing an orange-coloured envelope on a waiter.

"Oh, the telegram—the telegram!" cried Geraldine, clutching it in both hands with immense excitement.

But as she held it a recollection of her own dignity and of what was the proper thing to do came over her. She tried to look quite composed and unconcerned as she turned to Lady Mannington, and said in a very stiff little company voice, quite unlike that in which she had been giving the family history,—

"Will you allow me to look at this? It is a telegram from my brother at Oxford."

"Pray do. I hope it may contain good news," said Lady Mannington rather nervously; while her husband fixed his eyes on the back of the pink paper, as eagerly as Geraldine did on the front.

"Oh, I *wish* I could read it!" she exclaimed. "You know he's in for a scholarship, as I told you, and this is to say whether he's got it or not. It's Latin, I do believe. Oh, *would* you tell me what it means?"

She took it to Lord Mannington, and stood by him, holding one corner of the precious document jealously while he read it. It merely said,—

"Veni, vidi, vici. Wot larx! Home to-morrow. —TREHERNE."

"What *does* it mean—that he has got it, or that he hasn't?" asked the bewildered Gerry.

"It means that he has," said Lord Mannington, smiling in spite of himself at the absurd telegram, meant only for Gerry's private eye, "and it does him infinite credit."

"He has! he has! he has! Oh how lovely! how splendid! But it's just like Geof, and exactly what I expected. Oh *how* glad I am! You don't know how he has worked, and given up holidays, and got up early every day, and sat up in a great-coat, with two candles, all alone in his bedroom. And now he is rewarded. Oh, how delighted father will be! I wonder whether he knows yet."

"I should think so, certainly. I am very glad indeed about it, and I think he has behaved—I mean done—extremely well. When does he say he is coming back?"

"To-morrow. And father and mother come back this afternoon. And Violet's punishment will end to-day as well. What a lot of things to happen almost at once!"

"Violet's punishment?" repeated Lady Mannington; "come and sit by me, dear, and tell me what you mean."

Geraldine obeyed, seating herself on the sofa, as near Gyp as that unfriendly quadruped would allow.

"For going to Lord Mannington's, you know," she began, "and then pretending she was at Mrs. Ravenscroft's all the time. Dear me, how angry father and mother were! And mother cried—actually cried about it! Only think! And after all she never saw Lord Man— Oh, I *beg* your pardon. I had quite forgotten who you were."

She drew up suddenly, and turned very red.

Lady Mannington interposed. "I heard about it," she said. "Your sister thought Geoffrey had done something wrong, though I don't know why she thought so, and she took my brother for your gr—, for Lord Mannington, and told him all about it."

"Well, father and mother said it was a dreadful thing to do, and father said she must stay in her own room from that day—that was last Wednesday week—until to-day. So she has, and I *have* been so dull all the time."

"Poor child!" said Lady Mannington pityingly. "Suppose you come and spend this evening with me. You might come back with me now, and then you could make friends with Gyp."

"Thank you," began Gerry, and then stopped. Ought she to go, now her parents were away, and with strangers she had never seen before?

"Thank you," she said again; "but I don't think I ought to, now father and mother are away, though it is very kind of you, and I should like it immensely."

"I can promise you that she will not object," said Lady Mannington eagerly, reluctant to postpone even by a day the chance of making acquaintance with this newly-found grandchild.

"No; I am sure it would be wrong—thank you," repeated Geraldine sturdily, and to her surprise Lord Mannington seemed quite pleased at her firmness.

"Don't try to persuade the child, Maria," he said. "She is quite right—it wouldn't do at all. Come along; we must be going now."

He held out his hand to Gerry, adding,—

"I shall write to your father to-day, and I hope he will bring you all to dinner with me to-morrow evening. Give your mother my love, and say I am glad to hear that your father is better."

"And tell her that her dear boy has done it all," continued his wife, while Geraldine listened to these extraordinary messages with undisguised amazement. Just as her visitors were leaving the room, she regained her presence of mind and her tongue. Imagine Gerry without her tongue! She rushed to the bell and tugged it hard; then she ran after the departing callers, and said,—

"Please, I beg your pardon, and I'll give the messages; but what did you come for? I mean, to what am I indebted for the horror of this visit?"

She felt that this sentence was not absolutely right, but it was marvellous to have uttered it at all.

Lord and Lady Mannington went off into fits of laughter as she finished, and the former answered, as he followed his wife downstairs, "We came to hear about Geoffrey and his brothers and sisters, and you have told us. Don't be alarmed; you have done quite right."

Gerry had no further reply to make. She rushed like lightning up to her sister, and began to pour out the whole story as fast as words would come.

Violet waited until the very end, and then said,—

"Now, perhaps you'll give me time just to observe

that the people you have been telling tales of me to are your own grandfather and grandmother, and mine."

" Violet ! " ejaculated Geraldine, " what *do* you mean ? "

" I mean what I have said."

But not another word would she vouchsafe. So Gerry could only bottle up her wonder and curiosity until the return of her parents and Geoffrey that evening.

XXII

VIOLET MAKES A DISCOVERY.

EXACTLY at half-past four that afternoon Mr. Treherne and Lady Harriet drove up to the door. Of course Gerry and the little ones were waiting in the hall to receive them, and equally of course Gerry was the first to speak.

"O father, I hope you're better. Here is Geof's telegram—and, mother, mother, he's won the scholarship."

"Geof's collar—what larks!" said little Claude, as his mother kissed him.

"That's what the telegram says—out of 'Great Expectations,' you know; and Lord Mannington says —I forgot though, you don't know. Oh, I've got such *heaps* to say."

"Come into the library then, and say it," responded Mr. Treherne briskly.—"Let us have the tea in there at once, Harriet."

"How different he looks!" thought Geraldine. "What a wonderful place Brighton must be!"

And in truth the little breath of sea-air had done

more than had seemed possible.   Could this energetic, alert man, with the bright eyes and ready smile, be the jaded, listless being who had lain on that sofa a month ago, broken down and hopeless ?   The recuperative power spoken of by Sir Lewis —— had turned out to be a far more potent element than either he or his patient had imagined.

He walked into the library, and took up the pile of letters awaiting him on the table.   One of them caught his eye at once, and he threw down the others and tore open the envelope.

This is what he read :—

" MY DEAR TREHERNE,—Your little girl will have told you of the call which my wife and I made at your house this morning, and from that fact I trust you will be able to infer at once what my object is in writing to you now.

" I have long been secretly conscious that my persistent refusal to forget the wrong which I deemed you once did me, and to' acknowledge the manly courage, and ability, and conspicuous success with which, alone and unaided, you have fought the uphill battle of life, has been based on obstinacy and perverted pride, rather than on reason and justice, and that in thus acting I was ruining my wife's happiness as well as my own.

" But you have conquered now in the person of

your boy, whose fine qualities and high sense of honour make me eager to own him as my grandson.

"It is due to you, however, to say that apart from him you have well deserved that I should ask your pardon for this long estrangement, and beg you henceforth to let bygones be bygones; and it is right to admit that you have won for yourself a place in public esteem not unworthy of my daughter or of the hopes which I had formed for her.

"I have heard of your illness with sincere regret— it has been brought on, I fear, by an overtoil and anxiety which it might have been in my power to avert; but I strongly hope that the rest and freedom from care may suffice soon to restore to you your powers.

"One favour I have to ask, which I trust you will grant me, as a pledge of reconciliation. Will you let Geoffrey's future be my special charge? From what I hear from one of his late examiners, I believe he possesses talents which may one day make him eminent in his country, and I further think he has a noble straightforwardness of purpose which will cause his gifts to be a blessing to his generation.

"My wife and I hope that if you are not too tired after your journey, you will bring Harriet and your three eldest children to dine with us to-morrow evening at 7.30. We are fortunately alone just now,

with the exception of Harry Armadale, whom you
will remember of old.   Yours very truly,

" MANNINGTON."

Mr. Treherne was so entirely absorbed in this letter
that he did not hear a word of what Gerry was
saying.   She finished the first sketch of what had
happened at the same moment that her father finished
reading, and a spectator coming suddenly into the
room would have been surprised at the look of utter
amazement printed on the countenances of Lady
Harriet and her husband.

"Claude," exclaimed she, "only listen to what
Geraldine says.   They were in this very house to-
day."

"Harriet," cried he, "just read this.   It seems like
a dream."

She took the letter, and even Gerry was silenced
and suppressed by the sight of her mother's emotion,
as she read the words that once for all lifted the
burden of sorrow which had been weighing upon her
for seventeen years.

"To-morrow evening!" she exclaimed at last, looking up through the tears which dimmed her eyes.
"Oh, thank God, Claude, thank God, it has come
right at last!"

Just then the tea was brought in, and Lady Harriet gave her attention to that; while Geraldine, hav-

ing managed, from a sense of duty, to keep silent for about four minutes, began again.

"Lady Mannington—I mean my grandmother (how funny that sounds!)—wanted me to go back with her to spend the evening; but I thought you wouldn't like that, father. You see I thought then that they were strangers. And when they went away, I asked them why they had come."

"That was civil," observed Mr. Treherne, as he helped himself to another lump of sugar.

"Well, they had only asked questions; they hadn't said a word about thanking Geoffrey, or anything of that sort, until just at the end, when they sent their love to mother. I did think that odd, as I thought they'd never seen her in their lives."

"And did you tell them what you thought?"

"No, I didn't. I thought I wouldn't. But I did just ask"—here she assumed an air of importance and self-satisfaction—"to what I was indebted for the horror of their visit. I knew that was the right thing to say to strangers. But it only made them laugh. I don't see why."

Gerry's story had the same effect on her parents, much to her disgust; and the more so, as they would not tell what they saw that was funny.

"Lord Mannington said," she continued, in rather an offended voice, "that he should write and ask us all to dinner to-morrow."

"And so he has," said her father. "You must be ready at twenty minutes past seven. Where is Violet?"

"Why, upstairs, father. You know you said she wasn't to come down till you came back."

"Did I? Well, I have come back now, so you can go and fetch her down."

Geraldine did not much like the errand, but she did as she was told.

"Vi," she said, as she entered her sister's room, "father and mother are come, and you are to come down. And there's a letter from Lord Mannington, asking us all to dinner to-morrow. Father is much better; he seems quite well, and he is not a bit angry with you now."

She stopped from sheer lack of breath, and Violet rose from her chair.

"Do you mean that I am expected to go to-morrow night?" she asked, her face darkening.

"Yes, of course. Why? Shan't you like it?"

"No; and I shall not go. Nothing shall induce me," she replied. "I am too old now to be made to accept or decline invitations like a baby, and I certainly do not mean to accept this one."

"O Vi, don't talk like that, but come down, and forget all the horrid past. It's over now."

"No; indeed it is not," she replied. She very nearly added, "I wish it were," but stopped herself just in time.

However, she felt that go down she must. Her father and mother greeted her with a heartiness which set her more at her ease. The fact was that Mr. Treherne, now that the consequences of Violet's behaviour seemed to have ended, was inclined to take a more lenient view of the offence than had been the case before.

"Geoffrey isn't coming till to-morrow, you know," remarked Gerry. "Did he telegraph to you, father? He did to me; and the telegram came while Lord Mannington was here, and he read it to me. He said he thought Geof had done most credibly."

"Creditably; and so he has—my own dear Geoffrey! It is all owing to him that the grief of my life is at an end," said Lady Harriet. Then she added, "I think you two had better go now, and let father have some rest. To-morrow I hope to have the happiness of introducing you to my parents. They have asked you both to dinner."

"Not me, mother; I would rather not go," said Violet, looking rather defiantly at Lady Harriet.

"Nonsense, Violet," interposed Mr. Treherne; "you are to come, of course. You have been a silly child, and so I shall tell Harry Armadale—that is Lady Mannington's brother, whom you took for her husband. Happily, your meddling has not had the unfortunate results I feared, though that does not

exonerate you.   But you are to come to-morrow without any more fuss."

Violet's heart swelled with indignation, but she
dared not speak, or question her father's decision. Of
all the humiliations her misconduct had brought on
her, this of being publicly described as a silly child—
the majestic, self-contained Violet—seemed the worst
to bear. She shut herself into her room, and sat down
to think.   How she hated going the next evening !
" If Lord Mannington asks what became of his letter,
what *shall* I do ?   No one knows of it but me.   Shall
I say I never saw it ?   But that would really be
doing what Geoffrey said I did.   No, I won't do
that.—Every one is happy to-night except me.   Why
is it ?   Let me think.   Father and mother are happy
because they are going to be friends with Lord and
Lady Mannington again.   Gerry is happy because—
because she has nothing to make her wretched, and
no secrets to keep from other people.   And Geoffrey
will be happy because he has won his scholarship.   I
know he will be happy, too, because father is better,
and mother looks so delighted and so relieved.   Then
there's another thing.   Mother said that this reconciliation was all owing to Geoffrey.   And yet he never
tried to do anything about it; and I did try to get
him out of a scrape with his own relations—only I
didn't know they were that—but it did no good.   I
wonder whether Geoffrey has been right all along,

and it *is* better not to try and find out other people's secrets or meddle in their concerns.—I wonder what makes Geoffrey so much nicer than I am; for he *is* nicer, I can see that. It's not that he's cleverer or better-looking—I mean that's not the reason, though perhaps he is both. No; I believe it is because he is never trying to pry into or hide anything, but he just goes straight on in the way he thinks right. I really do believe it is that. I think I'll try and be like him. But then, ought I to tell what I've done? Oh, I can't! I can't!"

A voice whispered, "I can do all things through Christ which strengtheneth me." "With God nothing is impossible."

Happily for Violet, she listened to that voice at last, and kneeling down she asked forgiveness for her past duplicity and ill-temper, and then for strength to confess what she had done.

"It will be fearfully difficult," she said to herself; "but I don't see how I can begin to be like Geoffrey if I have anything to hide. He never hides anything, except little things, to tease Gerry and me, and those he always tells us in the end."

"Vi! Vi! where are you?" cried Geraldine's excited voice outside. "Do come and talk. I want to ask you such lots of things."

"I'm coming; you can open the door," she replied, in a voice which told Gerry that the "black dog" which had so long afflicted her was dethroned at last.

She ran in, an evening frock hanging on each arm.

"Which do you think I had better wear to-morrow?" she asked. "What shall you wear, Vi? You've been out to late dinner at Uncle Tom's, and I never have. Do tell me what happens."

"Nothing happens, except what you are accustomed to here."

"But, Vi, I never go down to dinner here. Besides, I'm sure it's very different. I've read about it in books. Isn't there a list of who is to take every one else in to dinner? And doesn't the lady or gentleman of the house come up and say, 'Do you know Mr. So-and-so?' And then you jump up and say, 'No; I haven't the pleasure.' And then he is brought and introduced, and you make a bow. I'm sure that's it. And then he says, 'Have you seen to-day's paper?' and you answer, 'No; is there any special news?' And then he answers, 'Yes; there's been a terrific earthquake somewhere or other.'"

"It seems to me that you know a great deal more about it than I do," said Violet, laughing and looking at Geraldine's delighted face as she rehearsed the anticipated joys of the next evening. "But, you see, when there is no one there you don't know, there is no reason for introducing people, and there won't be to-night."

"Oh, *what* a bore! and I had been practising bowing as Madame Michaud taught us, in front of mother's big looking-glass. Look, Vi, how nicely I can do it. You are a strange gentleman, you know."

She rose from the bed on which she had been sitting, held her pocket-handkerchief by the centre in her left hand, and made a very elaborate inclination, saying, in the stiff little voice she always assumed when she wanted to be particularly grown-up,—

"No; is there anything specially interesting?"

"But, Gerry, it *can't* be right to give the answer before you've been asked the question," observed Violet.

"No; I forgot," she responded, looking rather disconcerted.

"Besides, it *is* just possible he might say something different. Gentlemen who go out to dinner are not all run into a mould, like a jelly, so that they come out exactly alike."

"No; of course not. I know that, Vi. You needn't laugh so. I was only giving you an instance of what *might* happen," said Geraldine, a little hurt that Vi was not more impressed with her minute acquaintance (theoretical though it was) with what took place at grown-up dinner-parties.

XXIII.

EASTOVER'S RESOLUTION.

WHO does not know the delight of waking up some morning with a vague delicious sensation that something nice is going to happen ? At first you do not remember what it is, and you stay in bed, lazily waiting till the circumstances come back to your mind. As you lie there with your eyes shut, all that has happened and is going to happen comes gradually into your head, and you know that your first waking presentiment of delight is a true one.

This is just what happened to Gerry the day after her parents' return.

"Father is well—or at least he seems so," she said to herself. "Geof has won the scholarship, and every one will know how clever and splendid he is. Vi has got all right again. Geof's old lady turns out to be mother's own mother, and we are all going to dinner with her to-night. What a wonderful day this is!"

As she reached this point in her reflections she jumped out of bed, for rest and sleep had lost all charm in the contemplation of what was in store.

It was fortunate for Miss Newman that this was Saturday, and therefore a half-holiday, for Gerry was in a state of excitement which made lessons a sheer impossibility. She did, however, go through the form of doing sums, practising, and writing out some history. But every sum was wrong, without a single exception; the practising was so dreadful to listen to that Lady Harriet was obliged to appear with a message to say that "father would rather it stopped." As for the history questions which Gerry endeavoured to answer, the following extracts will show that they were not wholly satisfactory:—

"Who was Perkin Warbeck, and what was his supposed fate?

"He was the man who stabbed William Rufus as he stood in a doorway at Portsmouth. He was suffocated with his little brother, in the Tower, by Edward the Third.

"Name Henry the Eighth's wives, and briefly relate their history.

"They were all named Catherine, except the two who came in the middle, and were called Anne. They all had their heads cut off, except one, who lived too long. Her name was Lady Jane Grey."

Lessons generally ended on Saturdays at half-past twelve; but though it was a quarter to twelve when Gerry brought these answers to Miss Newman, that lady had no sooner read them than she turned to Geraldine, and said,—

"That will do, my dear, for to-day. You can look at these questions on Monday, and write the answers again when you are a little calmer. You need not go on with your lessons now."

"Oh, thank you, *thank* you, Miss Newman," cried Gerry, going to the door with a hop, skip, and jump. "And may Vi come too? We have such heaps to do."

"No; Violet may finish her work as usual," answered Miss Newman, who saw that Vi was trying to make up for her late nonchalance and sullenness by extra attention and diligence to-day.

So Gerry fetched her knitting, and tried to finish a sock for her Odd Minute Society.

She seated herself in the window, which looked into the square. Mr. Treherne's was an end house, and the door was round the corner.

She actually remained silent until the clock struck twelve. Then she heaved a deep sigh, indicative of the suffering her present self-restraint was causing her, and stood up to watch what was going on outside.

Suddenly she gave a little cry.

"There's a boy coming here—a big boy. Who can it be? It isn't Geof," she said half aloud.

No one took any notice, but she went on all the same.

"He's rung the bell; there's some one opening it—the door I mean. There's the door being shut—he must have come in. Yes; I can hear them going up to the drawing-room. Who *can* it be?"

Gerry was now speaking louder every moment, but she was still under the impression that she was quite inaudible.

Miss Newman and Violet continued their reading of "Minna von Barnhelm," without paying any attention to their companion's remarks. She continued to reflect aloud for some minutes. Just as she was repeating, "Who *can* it be?" for the sixth time, the door opened, and Lady Harriet appeared, followed by the very visitor whose approach Gerry had observed with so much interest.

"Miss Newman," said Lady Harriet, "this is Geoffrey's friend, Mr. Eastover, and I have persuaded him to stay to luncheon. I have brought him here, as Geoffrey is away; and I shall be much obliged to you if you will let the lessons come to an end now, instead of half-an-hour later."

Of course the book was closed at once, and Eastover duly shaken hands with. Then, as no one seemed to know what to do or say next, Lady Harriet observed :

"Geoffrey told us about the accident you had had. I hope your ankle is quite well now?"

"Yes, thanks," replied Eastover : "I'm going back to Eton this evening. I meant to go with the others last week, but the doctor wouldn't let me. I've had awfully slow holidays."

" I should think so," responded Geraldine sympathetically. " Do come and sit down by the fire. This is Geof's own particular chair."

" Is it? it's a very jolly one," said Eastover, looking very much at home, as he sank back comfortably among the cushions.

Lady Harriet and Miss Newman now departed, feeling that the young people—or at least two of them —would get on better if left to themselves.

" And would you like a footstool?" proceeded Geraldine; " Geof always has one."

Without waiting for an answer, she lugged an immense hassock across the room, and placed it under Eastover's feet.

" Oh, and you'll want a screen, of course; Geof always does. He says that great heat is injurious to the complexion and the visible organs."

" She means visual," observed Vi, as her sister presented the astounded Eastover with a many-coloured Japanese hand-screen. " Gerry is Geof's bond-slave, as you may suppose," she went on, seating herself in her own chair by the table and taking up some work.

" I wish *I'd* got a bond-slave," ejaculated Eastover, watching Gerry's next proceeding with great interest. " What a stunning fag she'd make!—Hullo, what's this? "

For Gerry, in her anxiety to do honour to Geof's friend, had fetched one of her Christmas presents—a

large box of French chocolate. This she offered to
Eastover, with the remark that Geof "was very fond
of that sort."

"Thanks very much," said the visitor, as he helped
himself with appreciative liberality. "So am I; chocolate is the one thing you can eat any amount of without its hurting you.

"I thought Treherne would have been back by this
time," he went on, quite at his ease now. "The fact
is, you know, I was floored when I got to your door,
because I couldn't remember his Christian name, so I
was obliged only to ask if 'Mr. Treherne' was at home.'
I hoped your father was Sir Somebody, or Mr. Ser-
geant Treherne, or something of that sort, and then
your man would know what I meant. But I suppose
he isn't, and so he thought I was asking for him."

"I see," said Violet; "but it doesn't matter. We're
very glad you've come."

"Yes, very," assented Gerry. "But, O Eastover—I
mean Mr. Eastover—what *do* you think? Geof has
won the scholarship."

"No! has he really? I'm most awfully glad to
hear it," said Eastover heartily. "I think it's a very
swagger thing to have done, and it'll partly make up
to him for leaving Eton."

"Yes, he does so hate going away; and I'm sure all
the other boys will be sorry too that they won't see
him again. Geof says they won't care a hang, but—"

" Gerry ! " interposed Violet.

" Well, Vi, I was only telling what Geof said. He declares they won't care a—a—scrap, but I'm sure they will."

" Yes, rather. Of course they will. He's a very popular fellow, and he has lots of chums."

" I said so," cried Gerry triumphantly.—" Do have some more chocolate, Eastover—Mr. Eastover, I mean."

" My Christian name is Harry, if you care to call me by it," said Eastover shyly, and turning very red.

Gerry instantly availed herself of the permission thus given, and by the time the first luncheon-bell rang, she and Eastover were getting on " like a house on fire," to use a favourite expression of Geoffrey's. Violet squeezed in a remark whenever it was possible to do so, but Gerry did not give her much opportunity of expressing her sentiments.

Eastover was immensely delighted with " Treherne's sisters," and made himself very pleasant—so much so that before he went away, at about half-past two, Gerry was moved to say,—

" Geof said that you were rather a croaking old kill-joy, but I don't see that you are at all."

Poor Eastover reddened again. He did not look altogether charmed at this report. He felt, however, that there had been some justification for it, and he answered,—

" So I was, especially the first day Treherne came

to see me; but I think he cured me. I pitied him then, but now he seems to me a luckier fellow than I am. I wish my sisters were as—as—jolly as his are."

" Oh, but," said Gerry, " it's because *he's* so nice and splendid, so—so good and perfect, and everything you can think of, to *us*, that we try to be a little nice to him;—isn't it, Vi ? "

" Yes, I think it is," she answered heartily.

" A little nice ! " echoed Eastover, as he thought of the arm-chair, and the footstool, and the screen, and the chocolate. " Well, I'm glad I've been here to-day. When I come home next holidays *I* shall try and be nice, and splendid, and all the rest, to *my* sisters ; and then I shall see if they won't be ' a little nice ' to me."

He departed a few minutes afterwards; and it may be noted here that from that day Mr. Harry Eastover visibly improved at home, and ceased to be known any longer in his domestic circle as " that dreadful boy."

XXIV.

FOUND AT LAST.

WHAT various feelings filled the minds of the four people who drove that evening to Lord Mannington's house! Geoffrey had not appeared when they started, so orders had been left that he should come on as soon as he could.

Mr. Treherne could not analyze or quite comprehend his own thoughts. A proud man by nature, he had bitterly resented his father-in-law's conduct, and even now, hearty as his letter was, Mr. Treherne did not feel inclined to rush too eagerly into friendliness and reconciliation.

"He has done me a foul wrong," he said to himself, "and Harriet too. I shall not make myself so cheap as to express any very exuberant joy at this change on his side. *I* have not changed, though he has. It is for the wrong-doer to change, not for me. He had no right to oppose my marrying his daughter so violently, merely because I had not a large private income. And as to his offers about Geoffrey, I detest them. After what has passed, to begin accepting favours from a man who has heaped insults upon me—it would be loathsome."

At this point in his reflections Lady Harriet interrupted him.

"I wish Geoffrey had arrived in time to come with us," she said. "O Claude, I am so happy! And to think that it is all owing to dear Geof! No wonder my father wants to do all he can in return. How sorry he will be when he learns why he has had to leave Eton so young!"

"It is all Lord Mannington's fault. If he had done his duty before—" began Mr. Treherne, and then he stopped.

What? Did he really think that to help in the education of his daughter's children was Lord Mannington's duty? If so, how could he be angry at his wishing, however late, to undertake it?

Ashamed of his own unreasonableness, and also of the contrast between himself and his gentle wife which her words had shown him, he said no more. But his thoughts were less harsh, and his resolutions less unforgiving, for the rest of the short drive.

As for Violet and Geraldine, their mental positions might be read in their faces, and written in two words —dread, and elation.

Violet still maintained her determination publicly to acknowledge all that she had done, when the question of the letter came up; but naturally every moment that brought her nearer to her confession made the ordeal seem more dreadful. Her mother's peaceful, happy countenance was her great support.

"She will be miserable at first at what I have to say," she reflected; "but then when she knows that I have told *everything*, she will be all the more pleased, I am certain."

If joys could be so used up by anticipation as to fail when the event looked forward to actually arrives, Geraldine certainly would not have enjoyed that night.

Dressed in her newest evening frock, with her curly hair as near being smooth as twenty minutes' incessant brushing could make it, she sat by Violet, with her face literally wreathed in smiles. Was not this the most exciting moment of her life? Was she not about to meet two new relations, whom she had indeed seen before, but only under circumstances which made the present encounter all the more thrilling?

"There will have to be explanations and speeches and all sorts of things," she thought, "and then just as Lord Mannington is saying, 'Now at last, beloved Harriet, I welcome you and your charming family back to my roof,' Geoffrey will knock at the door, and Lord Mannington will start forward, saying in heartfelt accents" (heartfelt accents did not seem to mean much, but what did that signify?), "''Tis he! He comes at length. My long and weary search is over at last. Welcome, my honoured young relative.' Oh, *won't* it be delicious—just like a pantomime !"

As she arrived at this conclusion the carriage drew up at the door. Lord Mannington met his guests half-way downstairs.

"Harriet, my dear," he said, as he kissed her with much emotion, "I am very glad to see you in my house again."

Then he held out his hand to his son-in-law.

"Treherne," he continued, "I have been wrong, and I own it. I never thought I should live to ask your forgiveness, but I do so now. It is for you to forgive and forget, if you will."

"I will," answered the other with deep feeling, and their hands met in the hearty clasp which means so much to the undemonstrative Englishman.

The drawing-room was divided across by curtains, as I said before.

Lord Mannington pointed to these as he entered the back drawing-room, saying,—

"Harriet, go through there. Your mother is waiting for you. I know she would rather see you alone."

Lady Harriet obeyed. What passed between mother and daughter after that long severance there is no need to relate here ; but when the others, some minutes later, joined them, though the eyes of both were tearful, many lines of care and sorrow had been smoothed from Lady Harriet's brow, and old Lady

Mannington had lost the querulous, nervous manner which had been the outward sign of her grief and loneliness.

Just as Mr. Treherne and the others went through the curtains into the front drawing-room, Mr. Armadale entered it also. Lady Mannington was in the act of greeting her son-in-law, and expressing her delight at the meeting, and Lady Harriet was watching them in silent happiness, so that neither of the three saw him come in.

He looked at the two girls who were standing very shyly together close to the curtains, Violet growing redder and redder every instant under his scrutiny. In a moment or two he walked up to her, saying, as he held out his hand,—

"How do you do? Are not you the young lady who told me that exciting story about Geoffrey and the dog? I think I remember your face."

"Yes," said Violet, speaking very low and fast; "but it was all a mistake—I oughtn't to have come. I'm very sorry now."

At this moment, to her intense relief, the butler announced that dinner was ready, and Mr. Armadale turned to shake hands with Mr. Treherne and Lady Harriet, whom he had not quite lost sight of during all these years.

"Now, then, which of you two am I to take?" he asked, as the other four departed, Lord Mannington

with his daughter, and his wife with Mr. Treherne.
"Which is the eldest?"

"Violet is," said Gerry. "Oh, how I wish I could
be, just for this once."

"Why? Because of the supreme honour of going
down to dinner with me? Dear me, what a pretty
speech!" he rejoined, looking very much amused, and
adding, "But I think, as the staircase will not admit
very comfortably of three in a row, you two had
better go first, and I will follow as your shadow and
obedient slave."

"And why hasn't the great Geoffrey come with
you?" he inquired when they were all seated. "I
have been hearing such wonders of him that I am
longing to make his acquaintance. I hope he is
coming."

"Oh yes, he is. He'll be here in a few minutes, I
think. He only didn't come with us because he
hadn't got back from Oxford," answered Gerry, who
had quite lost the vague sensation she called shyness,
which indeed had lasted only about five minutes.
"How astonished he *will* be to find us here! He
hasn't heard of any of the wonderful things that have
been happening."

Just then there was a ring at the bell.

"There he is," said Lord Mannington, who had
evidently been talking about Geoffrey too.

"Mr. Geoffrey Treherne," announced the butler, and

in walked that young man, looking very beaming and radiant, and the more so as he caught his father's eye, but withal a little bashful and uncertain as to what he ought to do.

To his extreme surprise every one in the room got up as he entered.

" What a disgusting fuss ! " he thought.

Lord Mannington came forward with great eagerness.

" Very glad to see you, my boy, very glad to see you," he said, wringing Geoffrey's hand as though he would rather like to screw it off.

" Ah, but I am the one to speak to him, and to welcome him," cried Lady Mannington.—" Come and let me thank you at last, my dear, brave boy, for your gallant action at the station. I never shall be able to tell you how grateful I am."

" It wasn't anything, really," said poor Geoffrey, quite distracted by all this effusiveness. " I hope the dog is all right now."

" Yes, quite, thank you, dear. You shall see him presently. Now sit down and have some dinner. I daresay you are very hungry."

" Well, I am rather. I've had nothing since breakfast but a very classical repast I partook of with one of the dons at one o'clock," he answered. Then he went round to speak to his mother and kiss her. " You look oceans better since you went to Brighton," he observed.—" I hope you are better too, father ? "

" Yes, thank you, my boy. I feel a different man," he replied.

Geoffrey saw his two sisters, and the longing look which Geraldine cast at him. " But I really can't go through any more functions," he said to himself, as he subsided into a chair just opposite hers. He tried to kick her foot under the table; but from the frown and sudden movement of the gentleman by her, he concluded that he had made a mistake, so he determined not to make that sign of affection again.

How it was that his parents were here—his mother looking so happy, and his sisters so excited—he did not in the least understand; but philosophically supposing that things had somehow come right, and that he should hear all about it in time, he began his dinner with an avidity which showed that his appetite was, if possible, more magnificent than ever.

Lord Mannington looked at him so long and so earnestly, that if he had been less engrossed he would have been very much embarrassed.

" Why, bless me, so it is ! " he exclaimed at last. " I've been trying to recollect where I'd seen his face the whole of dinner, and I couldn't recall it. But now I remember all about it."

" Whose face ? " asked Geoffrey, looking up; and

then, as he encountered his grandfather's eye, he looked down again quickly.

"Why, it was you who lent me—or rather gave me—the half-crown to pay that insolent cabman about three weeks ago, wasn't it?"

Geoffrey got very red, and said, "Yes."

"Now, Treherne, when you were a young fellow at school, wasn't half-a-crown rather a precious possession?"

"Very, I should say. It represented several important and interesting forms of nutriment."

"Well, then, don't you call a boy who meets an elderly stranger ('old buffer,' I believe, is the correct phrase now) being checked (modern expression again) by a cabman, and spontaneously presents his purse containing two-and-sixpence sterling, a very philanthropic and large-minded person, especially when he ends by walking off, and not even waiting to be thanked?"

"I hate to be thanked—it's beastly—I mean, most exasperating and unpleasant," said Geoffrey, with a clearness and emphasis there was no mistaking.

"You can't say any more after that, Mannington," observed Mr. Armadale, laughing.—"Now, I want to know something about Oxford. I haven't been there for thirty years." He turned to Geoffrey. "I wonder if it is much altered."

"No, I should think not, sir. It looks like a place

that has been the same since the Flood, but it's a splendid old town," said Geoffrey; and after that the conversation became more general.

Geraldine was too much absorbed in watching what went on, and in looking at her newly-found grandparents, even to talk; and Violet was far too nervous: so Geoffrey and his elders had it all to themselves.

"Come up soon, Ralph dear," said Lady Mannington as she rose from the table; and he promised that he would.

"Oh, there's Gyp! Vi, do come and speak to him," exclaimed Geraldine, as she entered the drawing-room, where that quadruped, looking fatter and crosser than ever, sat majestically on his own particular corner of the sofa by the fire.

"It's all owing to you, you dear, darling dog," cried Gerry, throwing her arms round him, but drawing back suddenly as he gave an ominous snarl, and opened his mouth in an ill-mannered and not responsive way.

"What is all his doing?" asked Violet, who even now had not heard the whole story.

"Why, our all coming here and making everything up. You know Lord and Lady Mannington have all this time been doing everything they could think of to find Geof, and thank him for risking his life to save Gyp. He jumped on to the line just as the train was coming. Just think how splendid!" explained Gerry, apparently describing an attempt at suicide.

"Is *that* why they wanted so much to see him?" asked Violet incredulously.

"Yes, of course it was—the whole, entire reason. But how they did discover him in the end I don't know."

"That is just what I'm going to tell you," said a voice behind her. She turned round with a start, and saw Lord Mannington, and the other three coming in after him.

"If every one will sit down, I purpose to tell them a story," he said, and his hearers wonderingly complied.

"Once upon a time," he began in a sonorous voice, "a grateful elderly gentleman and lady endeavoured to trace the whereabouts and discover the identity of a certain Etonian. But all their efforts were vain, and vain they would have continued until this moment, if Mr. Arkwright, once an Eton master, but now fellow and tutor of St. Austin's College, Oxford, had not come to dinner here the night before last, and told us an anecdote about the *viva voce*, which led me to ask the name of the youth who was the hero of it."

At this point in Lord Mannington's narrative the fire-irons fell down with a portentous clatter, and it was impossible to utter a word until they had been restored to their places by Geoffrey, the author of their fall.

"I beg your pardon," he said, stooping down with a very crimson countenance, and laboriously putting them up again. It was a long operation, and apparently Geoffrey enjoyed it, for he lingered over it an extraordinarily long time. At last, however, he finished, and sat down again in his chair. But his face was still a brilliant red. Thus thrown out in his recital, Lord Mannington had to stop a moment; but as soon as silence was regained, he went on :—

"Yes; without Mr. Arkwright I should never have found you out, Geoffrey. I can't think what made it so difficult. I saw you on Sunday, you know, and I sent my servant after you. He declares he asked your name of a young lady who had just been walking with you, and she said it was Geoffrey Montgomery."

"And so it is—and so he did," said Violet hurriedly and in a low voice.

Every one started and looked at her. She was pale as ashes, and her hands were clasped tightly together, but her face wore an air of determination, and as she evidently had more to say, Lord Mannington remained silent, looking at her in great surprise.

"I will tell you everything," she continued, her voice sounding very distinct in the complete stillness, "and then you will all hate and despise me. But

Geoffrey always tells the truth, and I see now that it is best. I thought he had deceived us about Lady Mannington and the dog. He seemed so anxious to avoid her, that I felt sure he was in some scrape. And he went out very early one Sunday morning, and wouldn't tell me why. But I thought I would save him from punishment by making it impossible for Lord Mannington to find him. So I said nothing about the footman asking his name, and no one else saw him."

"But I wrote after that. What became of the letter? I posted it myself," asked Lord Mannington.

A deep flush dyed Violet's pale face.

"I took it," she said, "and Geoffrey never saw it."

As she spoke she became conscious of a sort of murmur of disgust. No one spoke; only Geoffrey looked at his sister as if he thought she must have gone out of her mind.

"Yes," she repeated, "I took it. Of course I see now that it was—was—stealing, but I didn't mean to steal, and I didn't read it—not a single word, except the address inside. I just undid the envelope, and looked at that. And while I had it still in my hand Geraldine came in, and—"

"And you burned it. I remember now. O Vi! and I thought it was Ethel Barnard's letter," broke in Gerry, too much excited to keep silent any longer.

"I dropped it by accident," continued Violet, unheeding the interruption, "and it fell upon the fire; and then you came in and asked what it was, Geraldine, and I burned the envelope too, that you mightn't see it. When I had found Lord Mannington's address, I determined to go and ask him to forgive Geoffrey. I didn't know then that he was my grandfather, but I see now that I oughtn't to have gone."

"No; your conduct throughout has been deeply to blame," said Mr. Treherne. "It has been secretive, disingenuous, and interfering."

"Yes, yes; you are quite right, Treherne," interrupted Lord Mannington. "But let me say one thing. She has done her best now to repair the evil, she has indeed."

"And it must have taken a great deal of courage to tell all this to us," observed Mr. Armadale.

"I should rather think it must!" cried Geoffrey, springing from his chair and seizing Violet's hand.— "You've shown an amount of pluck, Vi, I shouldn't have given you credit for.—And I do hope, father, that you'll forgive her in consequence."

"Yes, do, please—*please*, father," put in Geraldine eagerly.

"If there is one thing," continued Geoffrey, "more horrid than to be publicly thanked and jawed over, it is to make a public confession of one's evil deeds."

"I agree with you, Geoffrey," said his grandfather; "so let us all consent to forget what Violet has done, and to advise her to follow your example for the future."

"*My* example!" cried Geof. "Oh, poor Vi! I'm sure I hope she'll have a better model than a duffer like me."

"No, Geof; in one way she cannot. For you have been as open and straightforward as she has been the reverse," said Mr. Treherne. "By-the-by, though, why did you go out so early that Sunday morning?"

Once more Geoffrey flushed to the roots of his hair.

"I only went to church, father," he answered.

He hesitated a moment, and then went on with an evident effort.

"I suppose I may as well say it out," he observed, "though I hate a fellow that talks about himself. But last half I was confirmed, and just before the confirmation I went to see my tutor about something. He wasn't in the room, and he didn't come in for some time, so I looked at a book that was lying upon the table, and in an American poem about an awfully splendid thing a Yankee did once there came these words,—

'He'd seen his duty a dead-sure thing,
And he went for it thar and then,'—

words that you see, even by accident, on a day like that, make an impression on you. I couldn't forget those two lines; they kept ringing in my head. And when I went to bed that night, I made up my mind that I would try to see clearly what was the right thing to do, and then, without thinking whether it was pleasant or not, just go 'straight to the mark.'"

THE END.

"Living to Purpose" Series.

General Grant's Life. (From the Tannery to the White House.) Story of the Life of Ulysses S. Grant: his Boyhood, Youth, Manhood, Public and Private Life and Services. By WILLIAM M. THAYER, Author of "From Log Cabin to White House," etc. With Portrait, Vignette, etc. Reprinted complete from the American Edition. 400 pages. Crown 8vo, cloth extra, gilt side and edges. Price 3s. 6d. *Cheaper Edition*, 2s. 6d.

Success in Life. A Book for Young Men. With Plates. Post 8vo, cloth extra. Price 3s.

The great principles of action which, under God, secure "success in life"—perseverance, industry, integrity, economy, etc.—illustrated by many examples.

"Yet There is Room."

Loving Work in the Highways and Byways. By Lady HOPE, Author of "Our Coffee-Room," "Changed Scenes," etc. Post 8vo. Price 2s. 6d.

"It is a volume calculated to stimulate home missionary zeal, and to suggest spheres of necessity, both spiritual and temporal, that lie immediately around us waiting the application of the powers within the Christian Church that have not yet been called into exercise."— CHRISTIAN LEADER.

Living to Purpose; or, Making the Best of Life. By JOSEPH JOHNSON. Post 8vo, cloth extra. Price 2s. 6d.

An earnest, practical book; shows how some of the greatest and most gifted men of the past have lived, and links counsels to their examples.

Living in Earnest. Lessons and Incidents from the Lives of the Great and Good. By JOSEPH JOHNSON. Post 8vo, cloth extra. Price 2s. 6d.

True "life in earnest" described in its various forms, with counsels as to study, health, amusement, etc.

Village Missionaries; or, "To Every One His Work." By the Author of "The Copsley Annals," "Father's Coming Home," etc. Post 8vo, cloth extra. Price 2s. 6d.

No Cross no Crown. A Tale of the Scottish Reformation. By the Author of "The Spanish Brothers." Post 8vo, cloth extra. Price 2s. 6d.

A tale, more of facts than fiction, of the plague in Dundee, 1544, and the life and times of George Wishart.

Records of Noble Lives. By W. H. DAVENPORT ADAMS. Post 8vo, cloth extra. Price 2s. 6d.

A most suitable volume for a prize or a present. Its object is to inspire, by graphic biographical notices of great and good men.

Masters of the Situation; or, Some Secrets of Success and Power. A Book for Young Men. By WILLIAM JAMES TILLEY, B. D. Post 8vo, cloth extra. 313 pp. Price 2s. 6d.

"One of the books which must be read .... Will be invaluable to young men."— SWORD AND TROWEL.

The Life and Letters of W. Fleming Stevenson, D.D., Dublin. By his WIFE. With Portrait. Post 8vo, cloth extra. Price 2s. 6d.

T. NELSON AND SONS, LONDON, EDINBURGH, AND NEW YORK.

Self-Effort Series.

The Achievements of Youth. By the Rev. ROBERT STEEL, D.D., Ph.D., Author of "Lives Made Sublime," "Doing Good," etc. Post 8vo, cloth extra. Price 3s. 6d.

Famous Artists. Michael Angelo —Leonardo da Vinci—Raphael— Titian—Murillo—Rubens—Rembrandt. By SARAH K. BOLTON. Post 8vo, cloth extra. 3s. 6d.

Interesting biographies of Michael Angelo, Da Vinci, Raphael, Titian, Murillo, Rubens, and Rembrandt. The book also contains critical and other notices by Vasari, Passavant, Taine, Crowe and Cavalcaselle, etc., which are both interesting and instructive.

Doing Good; or, The Christian in Walks of Usefulness. Illustrated by Examples. By the Rev. R. STEEL, D.D. Post 8vo, cloth extra. Price 3s. 6d.

A series of short biographical sketches of Christians remarkable for various kinds of usefulness, for example and encouragement to others.

General Grant's Life. (From the Tannery to the White House.) Story of the Life of Ulysses S. Grant: his Boyhood, Youth, Manhood, Public and Private Life and Services. By WILLIAM M. THAYER, Author of "From Log Cabin to White House," etc. With Portrait, Vignette, etc. Reprinted complete from the American Edition. 400 pages. Crown 8vo, cloth extra, gilt side and edges. Price 3s. 6d. *Cheaper Edition,* 2s. 6d.

Earnest Men: Their Life and Work. By the late Rev. W. K. TWEEDIE, D.D. Post 8vo, cloth extra. Price 3s. 6d.

Contains biographical sketches of eminent patriots, heroes for the truth, philanthropists, and men of science.

The Young Huguenots; or, The Soldiers of the Cross. A Story of the Seventeenth Century. By "FLEUR DE LYS." With Six Illustrations. Post 8vo, cloth extra. Price 3s. 6d.

Heroes of the Desert. The Story of the Lives of Moffat and Livingstone. By the Author of "Mary Powell." New and Enlarged Edition, with numerous Illustrations and two Portraits. Post 8vo, cloth extra. Price 3s. 6d.

In this handsome new edition the story of Dr. Moffat is completed; a sketch being given of the principal incidents in the last twenty years of his life.

Lives Made Sublime by Faith and Works. By the Rev. R. STEEL, D.D., Author of "Doing Good," etc. Post 8vo, cloth extra. Price 3s. 6d.

A volume of short biographical sketches of Christian men, eminent and useful in various walks of life,—as Hugh Miller, Sir Henry Havelock, Robert Flockhart, etc.

Noble Women of Our Time. By JOSEPH JOHNSON, Author of "Living in Earnest," etc. With Accounts of the Work of Misses De Broën, Whately, Carpenter, F. R. Havergal, Macpherson, Sister Dora, etc. Post 8vo, cloth extra. Price 3s. 6d.

A handsome volume, containing short biographies of many Christian women, whose lives have been devoted to missionary and philanthropic work — Sister Dora, Mrs. Tait, Frances Havergal, etc.

Self-Effort; or, The True Method of Attaining Success in Life. By JOSEPH JOHNSON, Author of "Living in Earnest," etc. Post 8vo, cloth extra. Price 3s. 6d.

This book of example and encouragement has been written to induce earnestness in life, the illustrations being drawn from recent books of biography.

T. NELSON AND SONS, LONDON, EDINBURGH, AND NEW YORK.

Stories of Home and School Life.

Stepping Heavenward. A Tale of Home Life. By the Author of "The Flower of the Family," etc. Post 8vo, cloth extra. Price 2s. 6d.

A tale of girlhood and early married life, with discipline and trials, all resulting in good at last. Every girl should read this remarkably truthful and fascinating book.

Ever Heavenward; or, A Mother's Influence. By the Author of "Stepping Heavenward," "The Flower of the Family," etc. Post 8vo, cloth extra. Price 2s. 6d.

A tale of home life, with its ordinary joys and sorrows, under the guidance of its leading spirit,—a wise, loving, pious mother.

The Flower of the Family. A Tale of Domestic Life. By the Author of "Stepping Heavenward," etc. Post 8vo, cloth extra. Price 2s. 6d.

A tale of home life,—the central figure being an unselfish, devoted, pious eldest daughter.

Changed Scenes; or, The Castle and the Cottage. By Lady Hope, Author of "Our Coffee House," "A Maiden's Work," "Sunny Footsteps," etc. Post 8vo, cloth extra. Price 2s. 6d.

An interesting story for girls, of two English orphans and their guardian, in the course of which valuable moral and religious lessons are conveyed by some pleasing allegories.

Almost a Hero; or, School Days at Ashcombe. By Robert Richardson, Author of "The Story of the Niger," "Ralph's Year in Russia," etc. With Seven Engravings. Post 8vo, cloth extra. Price 2s. 6d.

A Thorny Way. By Mary Bradford Whiting. Post 8vo, cloth extra. Price 2s. 6d.

A very interesting story, in which the character-sketches show no little discernment.

A True Hero; or, The Story of Amos Huntingdon. A Tale of Moral Courage. By Rev. T. P. Wilson, M.A., Vicar of Pavenham; Author of "Frank Oldfield," "True to His Colours," etc. Small crown 8vo, cloth extra. Price 2s. 6d.

A tale illustrative of moral courage, with examples taken from real life.

Aunt Judith. The Story of a Loving Life. By Grace Beaumont. Post 8vo, cloth extra. Price 2s. 6d.

A simple and touching story of the blessed influence exerted by a Christ-like life (Aunt Judith's) on all who came in contact with it.

Edith Raymond, and the Story of Huldah Brent's Will. A Tale. By S. S. Robbins. Post 8vo, cloth extra. Price 2s. 6d.

A curious story of the forging of a will, in his own interest, by an avaricious lawyer, of the immediate consequences of the deed, and of the peculiar way in which it was discovered, and the humiliation of the forger.

Follow the Right. A Tale for Boys. By G. E. Wyatt, Author of "Archie Digby," "Lionel Harcourt," "Harry Bertram," etc. Post 8vo, cloth extra. Price 2s. 6d.

The hero of this story is an Etonian who is possessed of a moral nature remarkable for its strength and power; and the book is written with sprightliness and vigour.

T. NELSON AND SONS, LONDON, EDINBURGH, AND NEW YORK.

Favourite Stories, etc., by A. L. O. E.

The Blacksmith of Boniface Lane.
Post 8vo, cloth extra. 2s. 6d.

A tale having an historical basis. Its hero is John Badby, the Lollard blacksmith, who perished at the stake. The incidents and characters are portrayed with all the freshness and picturesqueness common to A. L. O. E.'s works.

Beyond the Black Waters. A Tale.
Post 8vo, cl. ex. 2s. 6d.

A story illustrating the truth that "sorrow tracketh wrong," and that there can be no peace of conscience till sin has been confessed both to God and man, and forgiveness obtained. The scene is laid chiefly in British Burmah.

Harold's Bride.
Post 8vo, cloth extra. Price 2s. 6d.

An interesting story, written in the author's characteristic style, and affording instructive glimpses of the hardships and dangers of missionary life in the rural districts of India.

Pride and His Prisoners.
Post 8vo, cloth extra. Price 2s. 6d.

A tale for the young, partly allegorical, to show the fatal effects of pride on character and happiness.

Rambles of a Rat.
Illustrated. Post 8vo, cloth extra, gilt edges. Price 2s. 6d.

A rat telling his own story, with many facts of the natural history and habits of rats.

The Robbers' Cave. A Story of Italy.
Illustrated. Post 8vo, cloth extra, gilt edges. 2s. 6d.

A tale for the young. The adventures of an English youth among Italian brigands. With tinted illustrations.

The Triumph over Midian.
With Frontispiece and Vignette. Post 8vo, cloth extra. Price 2s. 6d.

A tale for the young, illustrative of the Scripture history of Gideon.

Fairy Know-a-Bit; or, A Nutshell of Knowledge.
With upwards of 40 Engravings. Post 8vo, cloth extra. Price 2s.

Fairy Frisket; or, Peeps at Insect Life.
With upwards of 50 Engravings. Post 8vo, cl. ex. 2s.

Fairy teachers (a sequel to "Fairy Know-a-Bit"), and lessons from insect life and natural history.

The Holiday Chaplet of Stories.
With Eight Engravings. Post 8vo, cloth extra. Price 2s.

Thirty-eight short stories for the young.

My Neighbour's Shoes; or, Feeling for Others.
Illustrated. Post 8vo, cloth extra. Price 1s.

A fairy tale, enforcing the duty and happiness of kindness and sympathy towards all around us.

Old Friends with New Faces.
Illustrated. Post 8vo, cl. ex. 1s.

A tale for children, in which some old favourite stories—Bluebeard, the Fisherman and the Genii, etc.—are introduced in an allegorical form, with incidents that illustrate them.

Parliament in the Playroom; or, Law and Order made Amusing.
With Illustrations. Post 8vo, cloth extra. Price 2s.

The Sunday Chaplet of Stories.
With Eight Engravings. Post 8vo, cloth extra. Price 2s.

The thirty-two stories in this volume are suitable for Sunday reading. Christian principles are taught in them without heaviness or dulness. It is a good book for the home circle, or for the Sunday school.

The Golden Fleece; or, Who Wins the Prize? *New Edition.*
Foolscap 8vo, cloth extra. 1s. 6d.

The Story of a Needle.
Illustrated. Foolscap 8vo, cloth extra. Price 1s. 6d.

A tale for the young, interwoven with a description of the manufacture, uses, and adventures of a needle.

T. NELSON AND SONS, LONDON, EDINBURGH, AND NEW YORK.

Good Purpose Tales and Stories.

What shall I be? or, A Boy's Aim in Life. With Frontispiece and Vignette. Post 8vo, cloth extra. Price 2s.

A tale for the young. The good results of good home example and training appearing in the end, after discipline and failings.

At the Black Rocks. A Story for Boys. By the Rev. EDWARD A. RAND, Author of "Margie at the Harbour Light," etc. Post 8vo, cloth extra. Price 2s.

A story the leading characters of which are two youths. One is always full of great schemes, which invariably end in smoke, and often bring their author into trouble and humiliation; while the other, a simple, unassuming lad, says little, but always does exactly what is needed, and earns general respect and confidence.

The Phantom Picture. By the Hon. Mrs. GREENE, Author of "The Grey House on the Hill," "On Angels' Wings," etc. With Illustrations. Post 8vo, cloth extra. Price 2s.

A story of two brothers and the misery brought upon both by one of them disobeying a command of their father. The innocent boy is for a while suspected and made unhappy in consequence; but at last truth prevails and all ends well.

Archie Digby; or, An Eton Boy's Holidays. By G. E. W., Author of "Harry Bertram and his Eighth Birthday." Post 8vo, cl. ex. 2s.

A very interesting tale for boys. The hero, a clever, thoughtless young Etonian, learns during a Christmas holiday time, by humbling experience, lessons full of value for all after life.

Rhoda's Reform; or, "Owe no Man Anything." By M. A. PAULL, Author of "Tim's Troubles," "The Children's Tour," etc. Post 8vo, cloth extra. Price 2s.

Martin's Inheritance; or, The Story of a Life's Chances. A Temperance Tale. By E. VAN SOMMER, Author of "Lionel Franklin's Victory," "By Uphill Paths," etc. Post 8vo, cloth extra. Price 2s.

True Riches; or, Wealth Without Wings. By T. S. ARTHUR. Illustrated. Post 8vo, cloth extra. Price 2s.

Teaches lessons such as cannot be learned too early by those who are engaged in the active and all-absorbing duties of life.

Culm Rock; or, Ready Work for Willing Hands. A Book for Boys. By J. W. BRADLEY. Foolscap 8vo. With Engravings. 2s.

It narrates the experiences and adventures of a boy compelled by circumstances to a hard life on a stern and stormy coast.

After Years. A Story of Trials and Triumphs. By the Author of, and forming a Sequel to, "Culm Rock." With Illustrations. Foolscap 8vo, cloth extra. Price 2s.

An American tale, the sequel to "Culm Rock," showing how well Noll Trafford, in after years, fulfilled the fair promise of his early boyhood.

Conquest and Self-Conquest; or, Which Makes the Hero? Foolscap 8vo. Price 2s.

A tale very suitable for a lad under fifteen. It teaches the important lesson that the greatest of victories is the victory gained over self.

Home Principles in Boyhood. Foolscap 8vo, cloth extra. 2s.

The story of a lad who, in spite of apparent self-interest to the contrary, held firmly to the principles in which he had been instructed by Christian parents.

T. NELSON AND SONS, LONDON EDINBURGH, AND NEW YORK.

Prize Temperance Tales.